Heartk

CW00435640

A N

Natalie,

Happy Reading

Much love

Content

Books by S.M Phillips

- Escape Down Under (DOWN UNDER #1)

- Fallen Down Under (DOWN UNDER #2)

- Forever Down Under (DOWN UNDER #3)

~

- Obsession (OBSESSION #1)

- Betrayal (OBSESSION #2)

~

- Since You've Been Gone

- Heartbreak's A Bitch!

About The Author

S.M Phillips is a fun loving mummy of two from Manchester. When she's not busy writing, you'll most likely find her head buried deep inside her kindle with a cup of coffee in hand. Talk to her when she's reading and things could get pretty colourful, pretty fast. Just ask her Hubby.

She is a lover of chocolate, especially if it has peanut butter inside and she loves a good cocktail or two. She often wonders if she should spend more time buying shoes, like most women, but then she remembers her beautiful never ending TBR list and realises that money can be spent on more important things...

... BOOKS.

If you would like to stay up to date with S.M Phillips, you can follow her social media sites below.

- **AUTHOR PAGE:**

  www.facebook.com/sphillipsauthor

- **TWITTER:** www.twitter.com/s_m_phillips_

- **INSTAGRAM:** www.instagram.com/smphillips_

- **GOODREADS:**

  www.goodreads.com/author/show/6987978.S_M_Phillips

- **READER GROUP:**

  www.facebook.com/groups/425452794259902/

- **STREET TEAM:**

  www.facebook.com/groups/1744600575786715/

- **NEWSLETTER:** http://wordpress.us9.list-manage.com/subscribe?u=51d2f0c4c8899acddced3eb20&id=15f50fbc85

For anyone who says that you can't, use that as your strength to show them that you can and you will.

Emily Parker's 10 golden rules to surviving heartbreak!

CRY.
Cry like a bitch. It's all got to come out at some point, so why not get it all over and done with?

DRINK.
It's perfectly acceptable to drink your entire body weight in wine, or beverage of your choice so long as it contains alcohol. Drink until you can't drink anymore, throw it all back up and start all over again. Hence the term 'Rinse and repeat.'

BINGE.
It's also perfectly acceptable to eat your entire body weight in chocolate too.

DRINK.
Now you might want to repeat step 2 again.

INDULDGE.
Buy yourself something expensive and pretty, preferably on the offending other's plastic if you've still got access to it. Failing that, break into your emergency stash as heartbreak is classed as a rainy day. Just think of all those tears. Go on, you deserve it. Plus, who else is really going to treat you?

EXPLORE.
Fully acquaint yourself with Vinnie the vibrator again. Lord knows you're going to need him on these long, cold, dark nights. Plus, he can't argue back so it's a win-win situation.

DRINK AND BINGE.
You might feel like repeating steps 2 and 3, so go right ahead. There's no one left to judge you.

DISCOVER.
Finally allow your best friend to introduce you to the world of online dating and turn you into a Tinder trollop. You'll soon be a raving addict and at least your thumbs will be getting some action. Hey, it's a body part after all.

CLOSURE.
Now that you've gained some strength back, you need to collect all of his belongings together and get rid of that shit. Rip it, tear it, burn it. Whatever you do, just make sure it's gone and remove every aspect of that prick from your life, forever.

BE HAPPY.
Finally, learn to breathe. Find yourself once again. Repeat steps 2, 3, 5 and 6, most definitely 6, to your hearts content, because well, who really needs a man?

Chapter 1

"Okay, you're really gonna need to order more of these bad boys after the day that I've had." I moan, throwing my bag down at the side of me as I let out a long, deep sigh; part frustration and part relief.

"Shit Emily, was it that bad?"

"Was it bad? Was it bloody bad?" She's got absolutely no idea. Seriously.

Bad is waking up in the morning to find that you're out of coffee. Bad is walking out the front door, only to realise when it's much too late that you've forgotten to put your knickers on and now you're forced to parade around commando for the rest of the day next to the office sleaze.

Bloody hell, what I would have given for it to have just been *bad*. I guess today I learned that some people out there are well and truly off their nut. It kind of makes me feel normal.

"You've honestly got no idea what I have just been through," I say, not quite ready to go into too much detail just yet. It's all still too fresh and too raw in my mind. Instead, I reach out and pick up another shot and throw it back, welcoming the sudden assault as the alcohol pleasantly burns its way down my throat, giving me a much-needed distraction. "What the bloody hell is my life, Rachel?" I say a little too loudly, just as the bar falls eerily quiet around us. I can feel the heated stares from the people surrounding us begin to burn into the back of my head. Great, absolutely fan-bloody-tastic. As if I've not been embarrassed enough today.

Trying my best to avoid instant eye contact with any of them, I fluster and end up slamming my shot glass back down on the table before me; albeit, a little too eagerly.

"You know it's only like three o'clock in the afternoon, don't you?"

"And... Since when did the time matter?" I ask my best friend as she watches me closely.

"It matters because you and I both know that you're absolutely shit when it comes to handling your drink, especially the strong stuff."

She's right. Of course, she's right. She's always bloody right, this one. But there's not a cat in hells chance that I'm about to openly admit that to her. "What's your point? You do know that nobody likes a killjoy, don't you?" I snap back at her.

I know that I'm being a complete and utter bitch, but why can't she see that I just need a moment? Now really isn't the time to start asking ridiculous questions. There is a time and a place for all that bullshit and in my eyes, that time's never. All I really want to do is quietly drink myself into a complete oblivion, which shouldn't take all that long, really. There's nothing wrong with that, is there? Plus, at least that way I don't have to remember how much of a Grade-A fuck up I really am.

Fabulous, now I'm bloody ready to throw myself the mother of all pity parties."

"Oh, come on drama queen. Put your inner bitch back in her box and tell me what happened. You seemed really keen on this one." She coaxes me calmly in her powerful soothing voice.

"Oh, I was." I let out a hysterical laugh as I remember the crazy butterflies that happily swarmed my stomach earlier this morning. "Ah, who the hell am I trying to kid here, Rach? Maybe I just wasn't built right or something."

"Whoa, whoa, whoa. Hold up a bloody minute. What the hell are you harping on about now you crazy woman?" Rachel, my best friend laughs at me. The one person who knows me better than anyone else is actually laughing right in my face as she tries to take me seriously, but I can tell just by looking into her warm and kind hazel eyes that she's failing... Miserably.

"Quit your laughing." I plead at her. "I'm actually trying my best to be serious here."

"Emily, listen to me. How the hell do you expect me to take you seriously when shit like that just randomly flies out of your mouth?"

"And this is the kind of support that I get." I silently sigh to myself. I give up, really, I do. When you feel like there's no hope left, it's just great when the reality that you're right just happily slaps you in the face.

"Rachel, think about it. Just stop for a minute and actually think about what I'm trying to say to you. It all makes perfect sense now…"

"It does? Well, I'm glad something makes sense to you because let me tell you, *you* bloody don't." Rachel cuts in, but I casually dismiss her concerns with a quick wave of my hand. We can always cover that later. For now, I'll just have to put it in numb terms for her.

"I always attract the fuck-ups. No matter what I do, where I go, they always come crawling out of the woodwork and find me." I say truthfully.

"Emily, all you need to do is quit looking for perfection."

"Excuse me?" My voice comes out on a high pitched squeak, one that sounds just like a pubescent little boy and my eyes grow wide as I not so patiently wait for Rachel's response.

"Hey, there's no need to shout. All I'm saying is that you seem to have raised your standards a little too high. So high, in fact that no one is ever going to be good enough for you. Look, what if one of these fuck-ups, as you so kindly like to call them; what if one of them is actually your one true soulmate? Honestly, honey, you'll never know unless you lower those goddamn high expectations of yours and give the poor guys a chance."

"Do not make me laugh. Are you actually being for real right now, or have you had a recent blow to that pretty little head of yours? How many times do I have to play the bad guy and burst your bubble of awesomeness, only to tell you that there is no such thing as soulmates? It's just a sad person's messed up dream, actually fooling themselves into believing that fairy tales really do exist. Honestly, Rach, it's nothing but absolute tosh if you ask me."

"Oh, Emily. One day someone may just surprise you and finally break down those steel walls and cut right through that icy, black heart of yours."

"It's icy and black because some little low-life suddenly decided that it would be a flaming cracking idea to openly claim it, play with it for fun, while somehow feeding his own sick and twisted pleasure," I say, very matter of fact and throw another shot back, only this time my head feels a little hazy.

"Oh hello. These little shots of goodness are actually quite naughty." I think to myself while watching Rachel eye me suspiciously, her porcelain heart shaped face cocked to one side with one of her flawlessly threaded brows raised slightly. I know exactly what's running through her head right now and I don't want to hear it. Ugh, I hate it when she starts to get all maternal on me. I know she means well and all that, but for crying out loud; I'm almost thirty for god sake.

I don't need mothering. Mothering isn't what I'm after. I need a bloody man in my life, a bit of fun; some excitement. God forgive me if I'm asking for too much, but a little bit of stamina and some pretty good sex wouldn't go amiss, either.

"I thought we agreed that you'd relax and have a little fun with all this?"

"Rach, trust me. As much as I would love to, and I'd really, really love to; there's absolutely no fricking way that I can relax and have fun with a guy who leers and groans, all the while playing with his nipples when he's talking to me. It's just not right." I add, desperate for her to understand how traumatic it was for me. "Some people might be into that shit, but it's not for me. And before you start, yes I know that's saying something. Like I said Rach, complete fuck-ups. Plus, he looked naff all like his profile picture either. I bet his bloody dick-pic was a fake too."

"Oh Emily, please say that you weren't…"

I smile a gleeful smile as I watch nothing but utter shock glisten in her eyes as they slowly grow wider and wider with each passing second. "God no." I finally say after a long, dramatic pause. "But listen, if someone's going to send me an image then you can bet your bloody life that I'm gonna open it. It doesn't matter if it's a picture of a cute little kitten or something that resembles a shriveled up portabella mushroom. It's being opened and the problem lies with the sender and the sender alone. To be fair, though, I didn't realise that guys still did stuff like that. I mean c'mon, they're not exactly the prettiest of things to look at, are they?"

"Ha, you're right, there. Now don't get me wrong, some do look pretty decent in the flesh, though. I just don't think that the vast majority have mastered the perfect angle or Instagram filter just yet."

"Dear God. I hope they never do." I squeal. "Can you imagine? Knowing my bloody luck my phone would end up glowing like Blackpool Tower and end up riddled with Chlamydia or something."

I can't help but shudder at the thought of seeing numerous pictures of a wide variety of man-meat. Jesus, it'd be a bloody cock-fest. In all honesty, receiving the odd dick-pic here and there does absolutely nothing for me, it never has. Bloody hell, if it did then I'd be googling the shit out of them all day long.

"You know you never said how you got away."
"Huh?"

"From the dude. How did you make your great escape?" She asks again, waving her cocktail glass around excitedly in anticipation.

"Oh, that?" My mind slowly trickles back to the present and automatically I dutifully reach out for another shot. *"Oh my poor liver, please forgive me,"* I mutter to myself before throwing it back. "I just politely informed him that I'd love nothing more than for him to stroke my balls just the way he was caressing his nipples because it was really turning me on and doing all things kind of crazy to me. I might have also told him that as far as I was concerned, the two of us were most definitely in business and I'd love to invite a plus one, obviously if he was into that kind of thing."

Rachel's drink squirts out of her mouth in the most ladylike fashion; from shock, I'm sure. "Oh. My. God, Emily."

"What?" I reply back and smile at her proudly. "If he can be rude and creepy enough to do that kind of shit to me, then it's only fair that I'm a little rude back, no?" Seriously, she doesn't actually think that I would just happily sit back and allow someone to insult me like that? Regardless of whether you know someone or not, bloody manners cost nothing and they'll always get you further in life if you use them correctly.

"Well, I guess I can't really argue with you when you put it like that, can I? But what would you have actually done if he'd ended up being quite partial to the sound of stroking your balls?" Trust her to come out with something like that. To be honest, that didn't even really enter my mind. All I could see was a weirdo sitting in front of me getting off on one. I just needed to get away from him and fast.

"Clearly it wouldn't have worked out either way for us, would it? I guess we just weren't meant to be." I laugh. I have to laugh because if I don't then I'll end up turning into an emotional freak of the week right in the middle of our local haunt, all because I can't bag a bloody guy.

"Fair play." Rachel nods and smiles at me and I'm almost certain, yet it could be the alcohol taking over my body, but something very similar to a look of sheer pride dances across her pretty, delicate face.

See, I knew deep down that she still loved me. Regardless if my inner bitch is out of her box, or not.

Secretly I think Rachel enjoys it more when she comes out to play every now and again.

Sometimes life just needs to be mixed up a little bit.

Chapter 2

"Hey Parker, feeling a little sexually frustrated are we?"

My shoulders tense and my whole body stiffens; one knee firmly jammed against the photocopier drawer to prevent it from swinging open like it does time and time again.

"Well, not today sunshine."

I bloody wish someone around here would have the decency, or at least have enough brain cells to actually get this thing fixed instead of trying to pussy foot around and just make do with it.

Trust me, when it's finally fixed, more work would get done around here and jobs that should be finished would get finished way ahead of time, instead of plowing through a constant bloody backlog.

"Please don't start Matt. Not today. I'm really not in the mood for any of your childish bullshit, okay?" I try my best to plead with him, even though I know it's in vain.

"Oh, someone definitely needs to get laid and fast." He continues, totally ignoring me, trying to push me as far as he can, desperate for some kind of reaction from me.

"Matt…" I say again, this time more affirmative. I've got an absolute shed-load of contracts to copy and keeping my knee pressed into this piece of shit is taking every ounce of energy that I have left in my tired and emotionally drained body. If I lose my grip now, even just a little, that's it… game over and I'll have no choice but to start all over again.

"Parker, you know I'll always be happy to help you out on that front. Any time, any place."

"Bloody hell, for God sake Matt, I'm warning you. Bullshit... not today," I haven't even turned myself around to look at him, yet I know for a fact that he's spinning around on his chair, smug grin fixed firmly in place, while he carries out his office clown act.

"For everything that's holy, God help me and prevent me from committing the mother of all crimes... Murder."

Holding my breath, I slowly count to ten, before finally exhaling on a long, dramatic sigh.

Great, this is bloody perfect. Now I feel like a right moody-arse cow-bag and that really wasn't my intention at all.

I love Matt. I mean, I really, really adore the bones of the guy. I might have even had the odd naughty and slightly erotic dream about him here and there too, but that's really beside the point right now and definitely something that he doesn't need to know about, ever. We've worked alongside each other for years now and he's been there for me through thick and thin. He's been by my side through some bloody amazing times, times where I've been too pissed to remember everything clearly, but he's also been a true legend and stuck by my side throughout all the messed up and not so nice times too.

I guess he's really a perfect example of all my needs rolled into one big human-sized piece of awesomeness, yet for some weird reason unbeknownst to me, he absolutely thrives from winding me up. The guy lives for it. I guess I'll never really know what sad little kick he gets out of it, but it must be some good kind of high because he does it all the time, desperate to get some form of reaction from me.

Usually, I'd be quick to take it all in my stride, always giving back as good as I got, but today the bitch is back and she's well and truly out of her box and there's nothing and no one that can stop her.

"Oh, chill out for a minute woman. I've got you a coffee here if you want it?"

"Coffee?" Oh, now he's gone and bloody done it, hasn't he? He's only gone and ruined all my willpower. But coffee, though. I know I should be a little mad, mad at how easily distracted I become at the mere mention of caffeine. I guess I just need to face facts and openly admit that I'm a major caffeine whore who'll do just about anything to get my fix. It doesn't matter how hard I try, I just can't seem to say no.

Sod it. Halle-fucking-lujah there is someone looking out for my sanity after all. Without so much as a hesitation, my knee instantly falls from the machine that's been holding me prisoner and the moment my foot touches the floor, my body instantly begins to relax. I spin around and see Matt watching me; waiting for me to take his bait with a cocky smirk etched across his rugged, yet dangerously handsome face. When our eyes meet, he nods his head towards the photocopier. The coffee in his hands has me hook, line and sinker.

"Giving up so soon, Parker?" He quips.

"Sod the contracts and hand me my coffee." Hell, I know that I need it.

"Jeez, Louise" He whistles. "If only getting you into bed was that easy, I'd be grabbing you coffee's all day long." When I don't acknowledge his ridiculous remark he smiles and throws me a cheeky wink too.

"Bloody hell. I suppose God doesn't half love a trier."

"What's the drama today, then?"

"I beg your pardon, drama… me?" I ask, one hand placed firmly around my coffee cup, the other pressed gently against my heart. "Why would you say such things to me, Matthew? I'm hurt." I lie.

He laughs his boyish laugh at me and gently knocks his shoe against mine. "Oh c'mon Emily. This is you that we are talking about here. Are you really trying to tell me that it's possible for you to have a day in your life that's drama free? That shit just doesn't happen and you know it."

"No, you're right," I agree wholeheartedly with him "but I'm still living in hope that one day I might just wake up to some strange, foreign, calm environment and I mean while I'm still living in the real world. Hey, a girl can always dream, right?" I add, more to reassure myself, rather than Matt.

I've been dreaming of a drama free day for years. I mean, is it really too much to ask for one day where I don't have to worry about being an adult and making sure that all the boring shit gets done? One day, one bloody day is all that I'm asking for where someone wants to take care of me for a change, to make sure that I'm all right. I've got more chance of Tom bloody Hardy waltzing through my office and whipping me off my feet.

"What are you doing here so early anyway? I saw you loitering earlier when I left the gym." At the mention of our gym on the top floor, I'm reminded that I still haven't stepped foot in the place all year, despite my daily motivational 'post-its' scattered about on my desk and the fact that I've scheduled an hour a day into my calendar for the foreseeable. Maybe I should look at asking someone if it's possible to trade my staff subscription to something a little more useful; like a year's supply of wine or something. It wouldn't be so much of a wasted staff perk that way and I would definitely make use of it, that's for sure. I make a quick mental note to jot that idea down on a post it as soon as I get a chance.

"Woah, woah Matthew. Are you my personal stalker now, or something?" I don't know whether I should be weirded out by this, or flattered.

"Personally, I'd like to think of myself more of a glorified bodyguard." I can't help the snort that escapes me. What the hell is happening to him? "Hey, what's with your face? Don't you dare sit there and pretend that you haven't been drooling over these bad boys." Matt flexes his biceps a little and I automatically roll my eyes at him.

Yes, admittedly he does have a beautiful set of biceps and yes, the intricate designs on his tattoos do catch my eye from time to time, but that doesn't mean I want to jump his bones, does it?

Men. No matter what anyone says, they're all the bloody same.

"You know that you automatically lose any form of attractiveness when you turn into a vain prick, don't you?" I ask flatly.

"Who gives a shit when you, Emily Parker, avid hater of man, have just confirmed what I already knew. You've blatantly just admitted that you find me attractive. Hey, you can touch 'em if you want. I promise I won't bite, well not unless you ask me to."

"Piss off and pull yourself together man. You're bloody more on heat than me and when you've been sex free for as long as I have, trust me, that's saying something." I groan. "Plus, don't you guy's kind of sort yourselves out on a daily basis? Morning glory and all that?"

"Forget what you read in those stupid magazines, Parker. A red blooded male has needs. End of."

So do women, the bloody sexist pig. Fortunately for me, I've got good old Vinnie to keep me company when I get home. I know, I know. It's not the same and nowhere near as good as the real thing, but what's a girl to do? It's not like I'm running around, batting all that eager and willing man-meat away like the plague is it?

"Emily listen..." Matt begins, but before I can remove the images of a monstrous cock-fest from my head, I catch a quick glimpse of glossy black hair out of the corner of my eye and inwardly groan.

"Bloody great. Today just keeps getting better and better."

"Oh, for fuck sake," I swear, turning my head to the offending object and I'm left with no choice but to take in the horrific sight that's stood before me; tall, slender, basically the body of every man's bloody dream. It comes complete with fake tits, teeth, and hair. Oh, and not forgetting a mouth like a bloody foghorn. Allow me to introduce you to Cruella de Bitch, also known as Amanda; my boss.

"Emily, are those contracts all up to date and on my desk?" She squeaks when her evil, soul-destroying black eyes meet mine.

"Not quite." I begin and already I can see her demonic powers begin to brew and build up behind her eyes, reminding me of a particular episode of True Blood. "The photocopier's having another bitch fit and I've been trying to fix it all morning too." I add, even though fixing the company's dodgy machinery isn't in my job description. I don't even know why I'm bothering trying to explain myself to her. That's not in my job description, either.

"I see." She snarls back at me, noticing Matt sitting rather comfortably next to me. "So, is sitting on your backside drinking coffee fixing it? I wouldn't exactly say that's being very productive Emily, would you? Is this what you usually get paid to do?"

"Well, it's exactly the same thing that you do, but you get paid a hell of a lot more than me," I mutter. What's good for the goose is good for the gander and all that jazz.

"What was that?" Her eyes grow wide, yet her overly enhanced face doesn't move as she continues to stare me down while waiting for my response.

"I said I'll get them to you before three."

Ugh, I absolutely despise her. She's nothing but a daddy's little princess. You know the kind; spoilt, bratty, bloody drama Llamas. What she wants; she gets, no questions asked, just yes, three bags full.

It just so happens that Cruella woke up one day and suddenly decided that she wanted to become all business savvy. But then again, who is daddy to disagree, or deny his little princess when she asked if she could take over this place? Thankfully, Graham still checks in from time to time and I'm pretty sure he still has the final say on any business decisions. It's a bloody good job too, otherwise, we'd all be out of a job and she'd have to kiss goodbye to her multi-million-pound inheritance.

Everything would be gone. All washed away, including her ridiculously dodgy fake tan and scraggly hair extensions. Actually, maybe that wouldn't be such a bad thing. Maybe the world would become a better place, aside from me losing my job, of course.

I guess money can buy you everything except class.

"I didn't think she'd be in today. Is this going to be a permanent thing, now?" I throw myself back down into my chair and pout at Matt. I'm not all too sure as to why because it's not like he can change anything or remove her from the scene, is it?

"Amanda's not that bad you know." He says quietly.

My head snaps up in shock and I look at Matt, my work husband for all intents and purposes in utter disbelief. "What, because she's got massive tit's and somewhere cosy and warm to stick your knob?" I snap back at him. What is this? He's supposed to be on my side. Team Emily all the way. I'm not asking him to whip out the pom-poms, but a little bit of support would go a long way.

"You jealous, Parker?" He asks, amusement ringing loud and clear in his voice.

"Seriously Matthew." I scoff, completely weirded out by all of this. "Do you even know me? Why would I be jealous of that? She's nothing but a jobs-worth, who just so happens to resemble one of those cheap and tacky blow-up dolls. Now that my dear friend is fact, not jealousy."

"I'm not too sure. You know that much resentment towards someone isn't healthy."

"And what would you know about that?" I laugh, moving my mouse a little to wake up my computer screen. "You're a bloke."

Matt looks at me blankly for a moment and then nods his head. "I guess you're right."

"I'm always right." I remind him.

See, now this is why we get on so well. He gets me, well, most of the time anyway and when he doesn't, the poor bloke isn't afraid to just nod and agree. It's bloody perfect. Honestly, he's perfect husband for life material. But then again, that would just be weird.

I look over towards the photocopier and groan for what feels like the hundredth time today and I've only been here for just over an hour. I guess I better get these contracts finished before Cruella comes waltzing out of her super, duper important office again. I'd really hate to end up being responsible for her *accidentally on purpose* tripping and falling over, or damaging her precious Louboutins.

Who knows, with any luck, maybe she'd end up with one wedged right up her fucking arse.

Chapter 3

"You're not going to believe this. I just know that you're going to love me for all eternity."

"I am?" I question, raising my neglected eyebrows suspiciously at Rachel. I've literally just stepped foot inside her café and in under a minute flat she's already assaulted me. Rugby tackling someone who's caught completely off guard can be classed as assault, right? She doesn't seem to care much, because now she's moved on, busily giving me a bout of vertigo as she jumps up and down like an overly excited little puppy before me.

"Bloody hell. All I wanted was a quiet break from the office and a bit of lunch."

"I think," she continues, completely oblivious as to whether I'm even listening to her or not, "no, scrap that. I know that I have finally found you a man."

"A man?" I reply flatly. "Rachel, what is he, a bloody unicorn or something? I'm sorry to break it to you sweetie, but they don't exist." Boys? Yes. Arseholes? Hell, I've met plenty of those, but men, actual real men? "They're nothing but mythical creatures. An Urban Legend, Rach."

"Well, I beg to differ." She happily shrugs me off, waving her hand dismissively in the air. "This one's really good looking and he seems to have a sense of humour too. But, just wait until you hear the best thing."

Oh, there's a *'best thing'* too? "Tell me..." I say, eager to please my giddy kipper of a best friend and take advantage of the short pause in conversation by plonking my arse down into one of the seats closest to me.

"He has a penis."

"No shit." I think to myself, but instead say out loud "he does? How do you know? Have you seen it?" My voice drips with sarcasm and I'm pretty sure my

expression mirrors my tone. What the bloody hell has she been on today? It's like she has a rocket shoved up her arse and I've no doubt in my mind that she'd give those Duracell bunnies a good run for their money, too.

"No, not in the flesh, more's the pity. But believe me, it was pretty hard to miss the perfectly defined outline of his super large knob in his extremely smart and dapper work pants. It was all rather quite distracting, really."

Right well, I guess that makes him bloody perfect then, doesn't it? One overly sized, perfectly shaped penis for me, please. Yes, having a penis is ideal, pretty much a necessity if you want to help add to the ever growing population, but from my past experience that's one sure sign that he'll just screw me over in the long run and not in the pleasantly satisfying down and dirty way, either. My current motto in life is: *If they've got a dick, one day they'll eventually slip.*

Harsh, maybe? Judgemental? Maybe more so, but it's the only way that I can protect my now broken and deeply destroyed soul. There's only one thing that I can rely on these days and that's Vinnie.

"Oh Vinnie, at least I have you. You're always there when I need you and you never let me down. No matter what, you're always ready and waiting for me. Such a loyal chunk of goodness good old Vinnie is." I think to myself.

Ladies, trust me when I tell you that you don't need any man when you've invested in an amazing and fiercely loyal vibrator. With Vinnie waiting for me at home, sometimes I feel like I can take on the whole goddamn world. Well, that's what I'm telling myself these days, anyway. Forget Horlicks, a little personal pep-talk can do wonders for the soul.

"Trust me, Emily, you're going to die a thousand deaths when you see him. Think Chris Hemsworth and Charlie Hunnam combined."

My eyes flash up to meet my best friends. She's been harping on and on, so much that her cheeks are now flushed from all the excitement. "I won't lie to you, that does sound quite interesting, but I bet he's still a prick on the inside. Plus, there's only so much excitement that you can get out of just looking at someone." However, if it was *the* Chris Hemsworth then I'd happily stare at him for a lifetime. Maybe stroke him every now and again too.

Yep, I'd definitely like to touch him, but can you believe that you can get arrested for that?

"Stop being so negative about everything. How are you going to meet someone, find your lobster if you don't get yourself out there?" She asks matter of factly as she sweeps a loose auburn wave from her face.

"I'm not going to be able to go anywhere if you bloody starve me to death, am I?" I moan back at her because, once again I know she's right. She's always frigging right. A ferocious growl from deep within my stomach makes itself known, cheering on the bitchy, hungry beast inside me.

~*~

It's been a while since I last stopped by Rachel's place. She's been harping on about getting the place done up for years. To be honest, I never thought I'd live to see a mass of new colour schemes and furniture. Kudo's to her, she's gone all out and completely re-branded the place for the better. It really does look amazing. In all fairness, I'm a little bit jealous that this little haven doesn't belong to me.

I remember when she first decided to open *Rachel's*. It all happened on one of our all too frequent piss up nights. We'd both stumbled across this derelict little shop on the way home and Rachel instantly decided that all it needed was a little love and it could strive. Personally, I thought she was going all Britney on me and I was petrified, to say the least. Rachel's never been one to stick to her guns and complete anything that she's put her mind to. Well, except devouring the whole Sex and the City boxset that I'd bought her a few Christmases back. That was the only time that she's ever gone AWOL. It was a pretty bad time for anyone close to her and I highly doubt that she even moved from the couch to shower. She really was that engrossed, the dirty cow.

We woke up the next day and sat down to revise her almost illegible business plan and she hasn't looked back since.

"Tuna melt for the grumpy cow."

"Thanks." I look up and smile gratefully at my best friend. "I promise I won't be as grumpy once I've eaten."

"Yeah, whatever." Rachel's elbow nudges gently against mine as she takes a seat next to me and I know that once again, I'm forgiven. I really don't deserve to have a friend like her.

"This place looks great," I say, holding my hand over my mouth so she doesn't get a face full of food. I know it's rude to talk with your mouth full and normally I actively use the manners that I was given, but I'm hungry and I don't have much time left to waste. The last thing that I need right now is Cruella hunting me down. Especially acknowledging me in public.

"It does, doesn't it. I'm so happy with how everything's turned out and the customers seem to be enjoying it too. It feels a lot more relaxed in here now."

"One question, though. Did you choose the colour scheme for me?" A soft mixture of purple hues capture my eyes as I look around the walls. The seats are plush leather in a deep cocoa and look so inviting. It's so pretty; it's so Rachel. You can't help but feel warm and cosy in here. I guess it looks like I know where I'll be spending the next few months over winter.

"How'd you guess?"

"Because you love me and this way it feels like I'm a part of you all the time."

"Got it in one, sunshine." She replies sarcastically. "Anyway, why've you ventured out of the office? You're usually strapped to that desk and can only be removed by force."

"Yeah, well." I groan. "Today happened and I needed the break." I wish I could go back to bed and start over, happily deleting the upcoming events as I go.

"Right, who pissed you off?"

"Where do you want me to start, Rach? How about everyone." Even I can't mistake the sound of defeat in my tone.

"Everyone?" Her smile dips a little at my words.

"Yes, everyone. However, you redeemed yourself by feeding me. I don't know, everything just feels off today. Like there's some massive joke that everyone but me is in on, if that makes sense? It doesn't help that bloody Cruella's back in the office. I really wish that she'd stumble over a bridge in those ridiculously large heels that she wears and does herself a serious injury." Rachel's mouth hangs open some and I know that she's dying to tell me off for being such a nasty bitch, but I don't care. "Add in that the photocopier's still being a fucking arse and then there's Matt. Well, Matt's just being Matt."

"Oh…"

Exactly… Oh. Staying home and watching re-runs of Sex and the City, surrounded by a monstrous bar of Galaxy sounds much more of a tempting way to spend my Tuesday afternoon. Instead, I've got to go back to that hell hole. "I used to love my job, Rach." I weep into my coffee.

"You just need a break Em, let your hair down and have some fun for a change. Unwind a little."

She's right. As always, she bloody right, Little miss know it all. "How much wilder do you think I can get with an M&S dine in for one?"

"You want fun, yes?" She asks and I give her a small nod over the rim of my very large - this could give costa a run for it's money - coffee mug. "Brilliant, because Thursday night my love, you've got a date."

Chapter 4

"Good evening, dear."

"Hi." I smile back to my lovely, old and completely bat-shit crazy neighbour. He's a lovely chap, possibly one of the kindest men you will ever meet by a long stretch, but at the same time, there's really only so much Grime pumping through your walls at all hours a sane person can take.

I was a little shocked that he wasn't blaring out the good old tried and tested, loved by all Foster & Allen, but each to their own I guess. God bless Mr. Jones, he's definitely one that's kept up to date with the times, that's for sure. I'd even go as far to bet everything I own that his surround system is, no doubt, every teenager's wet dream. It's probably worth more than all the contents inside his house, too.

"Make sure you stick that heating on and crank it up full whack, won't you? We've been forecast a week's worth of snow tonight." A week's worth? Really? "Wouldn't want a lovely young girl like you to be holed up all winter with a bad case of the flu, would we?" He continues.

"I'll make sure that I pop it on," I promise, my feet crunching against the gravel with each step that I take. "Speaking of the cold, shouldn't you be inside keeping warm, instead of…" What's he even doing? It's past six on a cold and miserable Tuesday evening in the middle of winter. I wouldn't mind, but I'm pretty sure he's almost clocking past seventy and that's putting it kindly, with all the love in my heart. He must be bloody freezing and I'm pretty sure a good old trusty pair of long-johns wouldn't even fight the chill.

"Don't you be worrying about me, dear. Red hot blood runs through these veins. I've got the body of an

Ox, or at least that's what Margaret used to tell me, God rest her soul. Plus, I thought it best to give these hedges a quick trim before the snow comes. It doesn't half ruin the scenery when they're all out of whack."

Like I said, completely bat-shit crazy. Who the hell goes hedge trimming in the middle of winter? Mr bloody Jones, that's who. I wouldn't mind, but there's hardly anything left on the bushes now anyway. Maybe he's got some weird form of twig OCD. Yes, that had to be it, twig OCD. It's a thing these days, right? "Well, make sure you don't stay out too long, Mr. Jones."

I'm almost at my door and I struggle to dig out my keys as my hands are completely numb. I can't wait to step inside into my warm, comforting humble abode and bask in my own little bubble. A bubble where no one else can enter without my permission. It's a pretty perfect bubble if I'm being perfectly honest.

"Oh, Emily." Mr. Jones shouts over. A visible cloud of hot air coming from his mouth, indicating just how cold it really is. "Before you go, I've got something for you." He waves his hands around frantically before scurrying off towards his porch. Something tells me that he wasn't really hedge-trimming. Or maybe he was, but maybe he just stayed out a little longer, patiently waiting for me to arrive back home. "The young Postman tried to drop this off for you earlier. Told him he'd have a fat chance catching you. I explained how much of a busy lass you are and that I'd be more than happy to take it in for you."

"Thanks, Mr. Jones." I eye the package in his hands suspiciously, trying to work out what it could be. I'm pretty sure that I haven't over-indulged this month. To be fair, me and my credit card have had a little to do and are taking a hiatus for the foreseeable. As hard as it is, I know it's for the best. When we're finally reunited again, maybe we'll appreciate each other a little more. Or, maybe when those nasty, power hungry control freaks at the bank take their goddamn knickers out of their arse and increase my limit.

"Here's a lovely shiny new card Miss Parker so that you can treat yourself to lots of lovely, pretty things, because you know, you're pretty awesome and you deserve it. But as soon as it's maxed out, we'll refuse to give you a credit increase because we're soul destroyers like that and we love nothing more than to watch all your new found happiness slowly and painfully leave your body.

Bastards.

"Early Christmas present?" He asks enthusiastically.

"I've got no idea," I reply truthfully. "but, I'm sure I'll have fun finding out."

I love presents. Absolutely adore them, almost as much as wine, but I feel rather confused when I look at this plain looking package. Usually, I can guess what's in it in an instant, but this one doesn't give anything away. It doesn't say what it is, or who it's from. All it has is a local postage stamp. That's it. That's all I have to go off. Who knows, maybe my Mum's on track this year and decided to send the Christmas presents early. I'd really like to think that, but this package feels like there's a heavy weight attached to it and not from the contents. Plus, my Mother loves to doodle, she just can't stop herself, so I'd definitely know if this parcel was from her.

It's hardly the most festive parcel that I've ever received, either. There's not one single Santa, reindeer or elf in sight. Instead, I've got a boringly brown standard package. I mean come on, for the love of God, it hardly screams *'open me.'*

I say a quick goodbye to Mr. Jones, conscious that my nipples could fall off at any given moment. I won't lie, I thought they'd gone on strike from being neglected for so long, but no; here they are, like bloody bullets painfully rubbing against my favourite *'double your cup-size'* bra.

As I shuffle through my front door, I flick on the lights and pop the heating on. Best do what Mr. Jones says. My house is small, but it's very homely at the same time. Cosy, even. It's a lovely little two up, two down that my Grandma bought for me just before she passed. She hated the current economy and found it shocking that young people were finding it extremely hard to get on the property ladder. So, instead of leaving me some savings in an ISA, she went and bought me a house. According to my wise old Grandma, she'd much rather I be set up with a roof over my head, than money that I'd only piss up the wall anyway. I'm glad in a way, It's not often someone my age doesn't need to worry about rent or mortgage payments. Also, every time I walk through my door, I'm still left with a little piece of her. A woman who I loved and idolised more than anything. No matter how crap my day has been, my little sanctuary always makes everything better, and wine. Wine solves everything.

I drag my feet slowly along the floor, my body completely riddled with emotional and physical fatigue and make my way towards the kitchen, my handbag clutched in one hand and my mystery surprise in the other. There's no way that I'm capable of saving this until Christmas. Two weeks is torture. It's a lifetime away. Anything could happen between now and then. God forbid I ended up in an accident and passed away. I'd never know what was inside.

I delicately place the box on my kitchen table, being extra cautious as I go. Who knows how fragile it could be. I remember one year when I wasn't so careful. The limited-edition penguin snow globe that my Mum had ordered from the back of her *Take a break* magazine shattered into a million sparkly pieces all over my kitchen floor. I was gutted, to say the least. I'd been hinting about it for ages too, and bam, in just a couple of reckless seconds, it was gone. Never to be seen or experienced ever again.

I didn't even get to shake it.

Chapter 5

I wake after a fitful night's sleep and feel horrific. I feel like I drank my whole body weight in wine, threw it all back up, gave no fucks whatsoever and then drank some more. Oh, wait, no, that's exactly what I did do.

I know that I'm in bed, my deep purple faux satin quilts confirming it for me, but I've got no recollection of how I ended up here. To be fair, everything became a blur as soon as I opened my mystery box. I can just about remember cracking open my wine and that's it...

Nothing.

What day is it? Please say it's the weekend and then I don't have to move and I can stay here and wallow in self-pity all day. Reluctantly, I roll over to the cold and empty side on my right and reach for my phone on the bedside table.

"Ouch." Bloody hell my head hurts. I press the home button on my shiny, brand spanking new iPhone 7 and shield my eyes from the slaughtering brightness. 8:55 am and its Wednesday.

Shit, shit, shit. I'm late. I'm usually in the office by now, at least three coffees down. There's not a cat in hells chance that I'll be able to make it through the doors in five minutes time. I won't even make it to my bathroom in five friggin' minutes.

I'm never late, ever. Today's already set to be a complete write-off.

Should I just call in sick? I've not called in sick since me and Rachel decided to go on a last minute trip to Newcastle. Now that's a night that didn't end too pretty, but that's another story for another day.

Why did I have to open that bloody package? Why did Mr. Jones have to be such a good neighbour and take it in, in the first place? Deciding that the world is completely against me, I drag myself out of bed and I feel sick. I've never felt so vile in all of my almost thirty years. Maybe one of these days I might just learn that I'm a lightweight and I need to calm it down a little before I do myself an injury, or worse; something I might regret.

First thing's first though, I need a shower. I stink, really, really stink. I smell like a student on fresher's week and believe me, that shit isn't pretty.

Almost an hour later, I'm showered, dressed and kind of looking a little more human. Oh, who am I kidding? There isn't any amount of touch éclat that could cover up these bags. Seriously, looking at my reflection, I feel like I'm auditioning for the part of uncle fester in the Addam's Family. Hands down, I'd get it too.

"What the hell happened to you?"

"I'd rather not get into it." I say, refusing to make eye contact with Matt. I must look a mess if he can see through my very expensive, but extremely necessary ray-bans. The fewer questions asked right now, the better. I can't even think straight, let alone talk to anyone.

"I wouldn't make yourself too comfy just yet. I've had orders from the lady boss to send you over as soon as you get in. I'll warn you, she seemed super pissed. I reckon you should have pulled a sicky."

The lady boss? What are they, pals now? "I'm saving those for desperate times."

"Emily, you look like a desperate time right now." On a normal day, I'd happily argue the toss with him, but I know it would be a losing battle. It's all Pinot Grigio's bloody fault anyway and that package. If it wasn't for them then I would have gone to bed a happy soul, but instead a depressed raving lush ended up passing out in my bed.

"Do I need to take weapons?" My head's still spinning and I can't be arsed with Cruella on your average day. Today, I may just get done for murder. Matt shakes his head at me, his handsome face full of pity. I don't want his pity. I want him to tell me that everything will be okay and I'm stressing over nothing like normal. Those words don't come and neither does the hug. "Do I have time to grab a quick coffee?"

"Emily, can you come to my office, like now? Do you not think you've wasted enough time already?" She shouts down to me. Who the hell does she think she is?

"Oh, fuck off," I mumble and quickly glance at the clock on the wall to see that I am in fact one hour and forty-five minutes late. If she wants to get all arsey with me, then she can call it me accruing my time back for all the endless hours that I've stayed behind over the years, desperately trying to amend contracts, fixing other people's mistakes just so that everything still flows well with the clients, and what was she doing? Off out spending Daddy's hard earned cash, because she sure as hell hasn't earned a thing since, or before she started here.

The door to Amanda's office slams shut and echoes around the silent office and it doesn't bode well with my head at all. "Is she being for real?" I ask myself out loud.

"Look, the sooner you get in there, the sooner you can come back out here and get on with things." I know Matt means well and he's only trying to spur me on, but he really isn't helping matters. All he's doing is working me up more.

"I thought you were supposed to be my friend?" My lips fall into a massive pout, one that could give Kim Kardashian a good run for her money, and that's a lot of bloody money too.

"Don't get all hormonal on me, Parker." He warns and it doesn't make me feel much better.

"Don't be a knob head then." I childishly spout back at him.

I don't bother knocking on Cruella's door. Instead, I decide to walk right in. Hey, if she can be rude and demanding towards me, then I'm not going to be using my manners and showing her any respect any time soon.

"Emily, take a seat." Her voice comes out snappy and her lips are pursed tighter than a cat's arse. It's not a good look and someone really needs to tell her.

"Look, if you're just going to be a bitch, I'll save you the job and walk out now." It's hardly a secret that we're not exactly bosom buddies, but up until now, I've always tried to remain professional around her. That doesn't mean I always have, but like I said, I've tried.

"I'm just going to get straight to the point with you Emily. I don't see any point in messing around. Don't think the work you do here goes unrecognised," Woah, what? Did Cruella just compliment me? Has she had a personality transplant in the last 24 hours or did I drink too much that I fell and seriously banged my head? "but don't think for a second you can flit in and out of here when you want. I'm pretty sure you didn't do that when my Father was here, so I don't expect you to do it now. Is that understood?"

Okay, definitely didn't have a personality transplant. "This is the first time that I've been late in years. Real life happens to us normal people sometimes you know." I argue back with her. I know I shouldn't, but she's just… ugh, I really don't have any words in my vocabulary that sum her up.

Her devil eyes move slowly from her monitor and she looks right at me, probably casting some kind of voodoo spell over me. "If you want to keep your job, then I expect you to do it properly and that means arriving on time."

"Not a problem, *Amanda*." Her voice tastes disgusting on my tongue and I think I could hurl up again.

"I'll make sure I'm here on time and I'll be making sure that I leave on time too. Was there anything else?"

"No. That's all, for now. Just so you know, I'll be keeping a close eye on you from now on. My Daddy may have been okay with you taking the piss, but now that I'm in charge things are going to be changing around here." Now it could just be me feeling a little worse for wear, but I'm sure there was a threat hiding somewhere behind her words.

"Well the feelings mutual Cruella. I'll be keeping a bloody close eye on you, too."

"How'd it go?"

"She's lucky she's still wearing her cheap tacky eyelashes. Who does she think she is? She's what, five years younger than me and she's speaking to me like a child?" It's bloody ridiculous is what it is.

"She's the boss' daughter, who just so happens to be overtaking the business, which in turn, whether you like it or not, makes her your boss. Plus, age means nothing, not unless you want to be done for discrimination."

"She's so far up her own arse. How can you be so calm around her? How can you even like her enough to sit here in front of me and try to defend her behaviour? You know I thought I knew who you were Matthew, obviously not."

"She's never really bothered all that much with me, to be honest. I quite like it that way. See no evil, hear no evil and all that."

"Of course she hasn't. What about when she comes strolling over to your desk, pulls one leg up so you get a quick flash of her flesh? That's really not bothering with you, isn't it? Why are men so blind when it comes to women?"

"Huh?"

"Okay, I'll say this once and I'll say it slowly for you. She's only nice to you because she wants to get fully acquainted with your knob."

Chapter 6

"It's so easy to use. I don't know how I didn't come across this sooner. You really need to get on here Emily. It's like my new addiction. Forget bloody candy crush. This shit is the bomb."

I've been sat at Rachel's, silently nursing my extra-large coffee, pretending to listen to her harp on about this and that for about an hour.

I won't lie, it's true that I feel like such a shit friend, and even though I want to hear all about her new find, I'm really struggling to stay focused. Not just with

Rachel, but with everything. I'm going to take a wild guess as to thinking this is what people feel like when they're stoned or on some super high strength pain meds.

"You swipe right if you like them, to left if you want to pass and then if they like you back you can start sexting. It's amazing. I've set you one up too. You're going to love it."

"What?" Her words suddenly pull me out of my hazy thoughts and into the here and now. She's set me what up, now?

"This new app that I found. Well, it's not new really, but it's new to me, so it's all the same. Tinder, it's amazeballs."

"I'm not too sure that I want to be focusing my attention on that right now Rach."

"Oh, give over. You're just hungover. Don't get me wrong, there are some right munters on here, but there are some hotties too. I'm already chatting to a few. You've just got to mull yourself through the slush pile."

"I thought you were busy shagging Doug?" At least she was the last time that I'd checked in with her. She seemed pretty keen on him too, but maybe he wasn't pulling out all the stops in the bedroom department.

Rachel isn't half fussy and she gets bored pretty fast. I'd go as far to say that an action-packed episode of Game of Thrones lasts longer that Rachel's attention span.

"Variety is the spice of life Emily." She states firmly while giving me her serious look. "Why settle for one man when you can have three? That's the whole fun of dating. No commitments."

If she'd told me this yesterday I probably would have been up for it, but now I'm not so sure. I feel emotional and a little lost and I hate feeling this way. I've not felt like this for a while, but now all of my emotions and hurt that I have been trying to hide and forget about for so long begin to ebb back in, festering in my delicate shattered little heart.

"I got a package yesterday." I blurt out, unable to stop myself. The pressure of keeping it to myself is making my hangover feel a million times worse. I'd love to have another bottle of wine, or five, but I know that it's not big or clever. Plus, I really need a clear head to deal with this situation.

"Has June been on a Christmas binge already?" She asks, not bothering to take her eyes away from her phone.

"I wish." Life would seem so much simpler if my Mum was sending me tatty novelty gifts." As much as I liked to take the piss out of them, I loved them really. It's always been her little way of showing that she cares. I guess it could be worse though, at least I'm not my Dad. I don't know how he does it. He allows her to go out and spend a shit load of money on crap and all he says is, "oh, that's nice, love." Anything my Mum wants to do, there he is supporting the hell out of her. Whether it's purely out of love, or just for a quiet life, I'll never know. Whatever it is, it works bloody wonders for them both.

It would be nice to have a little piece of that. Someone to love me and make me whole like my Mum and Dad do with each other. All I've got is my Prosecco, a secret stash of Galaxy and Netflix to keep me warm at night. Oh, how rock and roll. Life just doesn't get any better than this.

"So, who was it from? Did it sparkle?" Her eyes light up, full of suspense.

"Not so much." I've got no idea why I would have anything sparkly posted through my letter box. To be fair, the only thing that I get is my depressing credit card bill and my beautiful beauty subscription boxes. Maybe my credit card bill wouldn't be so depressing if I didn't get said subscription boxes, but then I'd never know what beauty must haves are out there just waiting for me to rehome them. "It was from Tyler." I say, numb, completely emotionless.

Rachel doesn't say anything to begin with and that makes me feel really nervous. Any minute now, she's going to go all ninja warrior on my arse. Why did I just spit his name out? Why, oh why? Earlier, I'd decided that if I didn't acknowledge it out loud then I didn't need to acknowledge anything about it, yet now, here I am and I can't take those words back. I could quite possibly kick myself, down an entire bottle of vodka and then drunkenly try and kick myself some more.

"Tyler?" Finally, she makes a noise. It's not really much of a coherent noise, but I know her well enough to know what she said. With a quick flick of her hair, Rachel clears her throat a little and says, "Tyler, Tyler?"

"Yes, Tyler, Tyler." How many other Tyler's do we know? Not many, unless she's keeping stuff from me. I so wish I hadn't said anything about it now, but I know that if I didn't, I'd only end up being sectioned or being admitted for a drastic chocolate overdose. What can I say? I like to eat my emotions. It makes me feel good at the time, then I feel like a fat walrus and then I eat some more to make myself feel better.

Vicious circle.

"What was it? What's he even doing sending you anything to begin with?"

"I don't know, do I? I don't even know what's inside it. I just saw his note and then backed away as if it was about to explode at any given moment." Just thinking about the memory sends my head all funny.

"I'm gonna take a wild guess and say that it didn't blow up, then? I know he's a twat, but I don't think killing you was ever really on his agenda."

"No, you sure about that, Rach? Because he did a pretty good job of killing my heart." I say glumly and straight to the point. I guess there's no point in trying to sugar coat the facts, is there?

Tyler. My Tyler. The only man that I ever loved; really loved. I mean, I actually loved him more than wine, not as much as coffee, but as close as anyone was ever going to get anyway, and what did he do? He fucking destroyed my soul and my whole life as I knew it. After him, the world tilted and everything changed. Now he thinks that it's perfectly acceptable to send me stuff, to my home address of all places, acting like he still lives there, or like he even has a place left in my life. Who knows, maybe this is the last Christmas present he ever bought me before running off into the open, gaping legs of Susan slag face Jones. Only I don't know why he'd be sending it to me now.

"I do miss him, you now." I confess. Me and my flaming mouth, it's always running way ahead of my brain. One of these days, I might just learn to keep it shut.

"No. No, no, no. You don't miss him at all. How on earth can you miss someone like that? After everything he put you through, too." Her lips form a perfect pout, but she's not for breaking eye contact with me. "Don't let some stupid little parcel undo all your hard work. You've been so strong this past year, you know."

"I have?" Bloody hell, it's not felt like it. I've spent the past twelve months heartbroken, only to pretend that I'm perfectly fine and life goes on, blah, blah, blah. But that's the good thing about alcohol and having a lush for a best friend. All these things can go by unnoticed if you're both shit faced all the time.

"Yes, you have. I don't tell you this often, or as often as I should, but I'm super proud of you. I just wish that you would have opened it." Rachel throws me a concerned look and I know that she'll have her phone attached to her hip as soon as I get home so that she can find out what was in it. I feel physically sick just thinking about it.

Chapter 7

"A house white, please. Oh, and make it a large one." I add, my voice small and weak. I briefly look around and even though this fancy, swag bar is almost empty, even though I'm rocking my favourite dress which hugs my figure in all the right places, creating curves that I never knew I had, and even though my make-up and eyebrows are completely on point, I can't help but feel way out of my comfort zone. I've even got tights on to protect my pins from the chill of the cold December air, and I feel bare; stark bloody naked. On show for everyone to see.

Looking down at my super-duper, brand new shiny smart watch I note that its 7:15 pm. Isn't it supposed to be the girls that are always fashionably late? Wait, no. Maybe that's just for weddings. Actually, scrap that, chicks are definitely supposed to be late all the time.

"Sure you don't want the whole bottle? No offence, but you look like you need it." The lady behind the bar asks. She's quite a petite little thing, wild messy black curls framing her pixie like face, emphasising her lip and nose piercings. Wow, either I look like absolute shite, or she can sense the nerves oozing out of my body. "A bit of Dutch courage?" she continues. Oh, my God, she can tell that I'm one of those Tinder trollops. I bet she's thinking all sorts about me right now. Yet, her smile remains warm and friendly as she waits for my response. Even though she's just insulted the shit out of me, intentionally or not, I can't help but think that the two of us would make awesome friends.

"Sod it. I'll take the bottle."

"That's my girl." She smiles, displaying a beautiful set of white teeth. She'd be fabulous on one of those adverts. Maybe I should tell her? Maybe she already does it. *Oh, bloody hell Emily, now your floundering.* "Go take a seat and I'll bring it over for you."

After thanking my new Pixie-ish friend, I look around the empty bar and quickly weigh up my options. Should I take a window seat so it's easier for a quick getaway, but then at the same time I'd be allowing the whole of Soho to witness how pathetic I am once I've been stood up, or should I take the cosy, romantic booth, where I run a high risk of being hidden away by some crazed psycho, unable to cry out for help?

Deciding that I'd rather not embarrass myself by allowing the lovely folks of London to witness me drinking alone, whilst swiping through my possible matches on Tinder to pass the time, I take the plunge with fate, hoping and praying that this Noah guy isn't some mass serial killer.

My phone chimes to life just as I wiggle my arse into a cosy corner booth. I take another look around me before rummaging in my bag and quickly pull out my phone and see that it's a message from Rachel.

So, how's the date going? Told you he was edible, didn't I? You jumped his bones yet? Have you at least licked his face? God, I so wish I was you, you lucky cow.

What date? I tap out hastily. *He isn't even here yet.*

Oh, God. I hope this isn't some practical joke on my part. What if Rachel's set me up? I feel like I'm about to be punked. Is this the reason why the place is dead? I can just imagine all the hidden cameras zooming in at me from every possible unsightly angle right now. I'd like to think that Rachel wouldn't stoop so low, because that would be down, right evil, but then everyone's got an evil streak in them somewhere, haven't they? I'll admit that I'm yet to find mine. If this is the case, then I'm afraid to say that Rachel's going to need to find a new best friend and fast. Oh, and she'll also need to hire some pretty good security too.

"Erm… excuse me Miss, are you Emily?" A deep, rustic voice pulls my eyes away from my phone, Tinder still open. I really have no shame. I look up slowly, dreading that a massive camera will be planted in my face.

"Holy fucking shit." I blink a few times and I know that my mouth is hanging wide open, but jeez Louise. A seriously hot, fine specimen of a man is leaning over and looking right at me. Shit, I can't breathe. Why can't I breathe? He's like some mythical creature who's removed my ability to carry out any human functions. "ummm…" I just about manage as he extends his hand out to mine.

"I'm Noah."

Everything happens so quickly. One minute my hand is protectively holding my phone, the next my palm becomes quite clammy and as I lift my hand out to shake his, my brain forgets that my phone exists and it goes flying across the table, only to land with a huge thud, I hear the shatter of glass and we both look towards my poor, innocent, now broken phone, and what can this God of all sins see? My flaming Tinder app, wide open inviting the whole world to take a little look, acting like the little slut face it really is.

"Ouch." He says, his plump bottom lip protruding.

Bloody ouch is right. I don't know what to be more pissed off about, the fact that my phone's broken or the fact that I didn't have enough bloody brain cells to close out of that app, before hot stuff saw it. I told Rachel

I didn't want to be on Tinder. I told her that nothing good could ever come from it, apart from my right thumb becoming a swipe whore. But would she listen? Would she bloody hell as like.

I hate to admit that as soon as I took a quick look, my curious mind getting the better of me and had my first swipe, that was it. It was game over for me. I was addicted and it wasn't my fault. It was Rachel's, all Rachel's. And now, because she's set me up with this hottie, I'm going to lay the blame on her too for my broken phone. The bitch needs to know that she owes me a new iPhone 7 and a whole new identity.

"Nah, don't worry about it. Happens all the time." I reply quickly, my mouth shooting off before I can stop it.

"Good to know." He half smiles. I don't know this guy from Adam, oh, how I'd like to, but my instincts are telling me that he's feeling a little uncomfortable. "Mind if I take a seat?"

"Sure. I don't mean that," I say, pointing to some random guy's face lit up on my screen, just about hidden from the shattered glass. The last thing I want is for him to think I'm some cock hungry little hussy. No, that would be Susan and the rest of the plastics that go out to devour the cock. Honestly, I wouldn't even be able to tell you if he was worth a like, the screens that shattered he looks like he's been stuck inside one of those kaleidoscope thingy-majigs. "I'm pretty clumsy when it comes to my belongings." Correction, I'm clumsy when something knocks me off guard and this beauty has definitely done that.

To be fair to Rachel, she wasn't lying when she said he looked like Chris Hemsworth. This guy's his doppelganger for sure, from the heavy set of his broad shoulders, Thor style, right down to his thick main of dirty blonde hair. I've got to be dreaming, there's no way that I'm out on a date with Thor. Hell, he might not be the real deal, but trust me when I tell you it's the closest to a Hemsworth that anyone's going to get. Sticking the two of them together, even Liam would start demanding a DNA test.

"So I can see. Myself and Apple don't see eye to eye. Too much of their shit has messed up on me in the past."

Oh no, please don't say that. Please stop talking. He's only been here for what, less than five minutes and already we have differences of opinion. Now it's off to bad start.

Even though he's just gone down a notch in my book, well, you really can't say things like that to an apple whore and expect them to like you, even if what they're saying is true. It just doesn't happen. Saying that though, I still can't pull my eyes away from him. He's just so... manly. He's oozing pure testosterone. Biting down on my lower lip, I have to resist the urge to reach out and touch him. Purely just to see what he feels like. This is fucking crazy. "Can I get you a drink?" He asks, bringing me back to my senses.

"Here you go, my love." My new found friend suddenly appears behind my Thor just as I'm about to answer him. "Here's your bottle, and I've thrown in a large white for you too." She beams at me, clearly thinking that she's doing me a favour, then tilts her head towards Noah and mouths *"wow"* over his shoulder. Wow is right, but we're not going to be friends if she carries on making out that I'm some raging Lush. Then again, I guess she'd be right. "Can I get something for you?" She asks, before heading back to the bar.

"Just a bottle of beer for me, thanks." Noah leans back in the booth, his legs so long and muscular that his knees are almost touching the table and his legs are sticking out from the sides. Jesus, he's fucking perfect. All kinds of crazy images are running wild in my head right now. I'm even shocked at my own imagination. *Pull it back Emily and get your head out of the gutter.*

The question is, what the hell is he doing here with me? Now that's something that I can't seem to get my head around. "So how do you know Rachel?" I ask, once again curiosity getting the better of me. Knowing Rachel, there's a high possibility that she doesn't even know him, she's just stalked and pecked him long enough to bag me a date. More importantly though, how is he even single?

"I'm pretty much a regular at her place." He says and the words just casually slip off his tongue.

"You are?" I ask, slightly confused.

"Oh, not like that. I mean her coffee shop, not her actual place." His voice comes across more forceful as he tells me this, and he seems adamant to make that little bit of information clear. Yet, a warm glow heats his face.

From embarrassment? Maybe we're not so different after all. Now there's the plus that I've been looking for.

"If you were a regular at her house, trust me, I'd know all about you by now. Every teeny, tiny little thing, right down to your shoe size. She's got a way of getting right down to the nitty gritty with people. I guess you could say it's one of her many charms."

We spend the rest of our date making small talk and finding out more about each other. I'm quite surprised actually. Considering he's so good looking and he must know it too, he's not arrogant at all. Yes, I know you shouldn't judge people before you know them, but what can you do when the majority of the male population are utter bell-ends?

Chapter 8

"Emily. Hello, are you there?"

"Huh? Did you say something?" Rachel looks at me gormlessly, which isn't anything out of the ordinary to be fair. She's always looked at me as if I'm from another planet. Why I guess I'll never know "What?" Why is she smiling at me like that? Now she's making me feel really uneasy. All I want to do is grab a quick coffee before heading to work. Instead, she looks like she's taken some kind or legal or maybe not so legal high and she's happily playing away with the fairies.

"I'm going to take that as a big fat yes, then. I knew it. Just call me this generation's Cilla." She gleefully chimes down my ear.

"What are you jabbering on about now? It's early and I need my coffee Rachel." I warn.

"Noah, you fool."

Oh, Noah. My mind wanders back to him. Back to the place that it's been since last night. In the flaming gutter. I woke up this morning and thought that I'd dreamt it all. Every last bit of it. I was totally convinced that he was just a figment of my imagination, that was until my phone buzzed to life, and there he was, my very own Thor, crashing through my overly damaged phone, zapping all my energy away like the real Thor does with the air, before pummelling all his hot, steamy rage down on you. Oh, how I would so love for that to happen in real life.

"Take your bloody mind out of the gutter, Emily. Jesus Christ, there's only so much your poor heart can take so early on a Friday morning. Especially without your usual hit of caffeine."

I'm fully aware that a large queue is beginning to form behind me and I know that now isn't really the place to be getting into this kind of conversation. I know my best friend though and I know that she isn't going to let this drop until I spill the beans to her. She's a right nosey cow like that. It's a bloody good job that I love her. "How about we meet for lunch? It'll give us more time to talk then. You know, away from prying eyes and ears?" I add loudly.

She hands me my coffee but doesn't break eye contact with me and I know she's trying to pull the answers from my mind. "So there's much to discuss, then?"

"Not really but you'll just have to wait and see. Plus, anticipation is good for the soul so they say."

"You'll tell me anything. Be here for one-ish? I'll be able to sneak off around that time."

I can hear a not so silent huff behind me and my head whips around. "I'm almost done, so calm your arse. It's no wonder you're not getting laid with an attitude like that." I snap at the sour, middle-aged man stood behind me. Rachel looks at me with raised eyebrows and I know that I've overstepped the mark a little. I hate people being rude, though, it really grates on me, but I really need to remember where I am at times. Rachel's pride and joy is not somewhere that I should be starting a hoe-down show-down. I mouth a quick apology to her and grab my bagel. "One o'clock. I'll be here." I promise and I quickly dart out of the door.

The office is surprisingly quiet for a Friday morning. Even Cruella doesn't look like she's risen from her lair, yet. Maybe today might just be a good day after all. No whining, no bitching, just pure bliss, just me and my thoughts.

First things first, though. I need to enjoy my coffee before I can even contemplate doing any work. I take a sip and realise I'm going to need to drink it quickly before it turns into a poor man's frappe. I mean come on, priorities and all that.

I scan the office around me once more as I patiently wait for my computer to come out of its coma. I sit and wait patiently. Still, nothing and it's all a little strange. I'm shocked that Matt isn't loitering around like he usually does. Does that man even sleep? I glance at the clock and it's almost 9 am and no one's here. Something's definitely off, I just don't know what, yet.

Where are you? Are you sick, or are you sick-sick? I quickly type out to Matt. The latter being that I'm a nosey bitch and I need to know if he got lucky last night. Maybe he's really ill and he's come down with man flu. Oh, bloody hell, I hope that's not the case. If it is, then I'm never going to hear the end of it. A man with a cold is horrific. They act like the slightest sneeze will take them over the edge, destined never to breathe life ever again. I don't know what it is, but men don't half turn into horrific, hot messes when they've got just a sniffle. God only knows how they would react if they ended up having to deal with period cramps and dare I say it, childbirth?

"Oh, you're already here. Good. I wasn't all too sure if you'd received my memo."

"Erm… hey. What memo?" I ask, slightly confused. Standing across from me is my boss. My real boss. The guy who actually pays my wages, not the little floozy who tries to waste them.

Graham looks as superior as ever. Nothing out of place, everything prim and proper. He would have made a wonderful gangster, but I guess that's for another day.

Though he may have aged over the years, he's sure aged gracefully. Think sexy, silver fox. Think George Clooney, Phillip Schofield and the like. I'm about to ask some more questions when my phone buzzes loudly on my desk, interrupting my train of thought. I chance a quick peek and see a short and sweet reply from Matt.

Good luck, Parker.

Good luck? Why would he be wishing me luck? I'm the only one who's rocked up at the office on time. If anything, he's the one that's going to need some luck. I swear if he's been at my desk and mauled my stuff, happily spreading his germs, then he's going to suffer a long and painful death at my own hands. I hate being ill. There's nothing worse, well except when The Great British Bake off ends. That makes me feel ill, and a bit depressed and completely lost.

"Come on then, I don't think you want to keep me waiting, do you?" He snaps and it's not a familiar tone that I'm used to with Graham. Over the years, we've always had a good, solid work relationship. Could it be possible that he's just having a bad day? I bloody hope so.

"Graham, what's this about? You were the last person that I expected to see today." I say, nervously. I feel physically sick and my gut is telling me to steer well clear of where this is going. Everything about this whole situation just smells off.

"I can see that. Let's get this over and done with, shall we? My office, now." He doesn't look at me, he doesn't even wait for me to get up. Instead, he turns on his designer-clad foot and walks away from me, and there's not a single smile in sight.

Why do I get the sudden feeling that I've done something wrong? I know I haven't, but now I feel like I've been a naughty little school girl and now I'm being marched down to the headmaster's office to receive my punishment. I'm so confused. There's been nothing wrong with my work, and my work pile has been empty for weeks. If anything, I've been busy clearing everyone else's and what, this is the thanks I get? Being spoken to like a piece of shit from my boss, boss.

Realising I've not really got much choice in the matter, I gracefully stand and smooth down my pencil skirt, before dutifully following his lead. Not that I want to, I'd much rather throw a monstrous temper tantrum, screaming out really loud until it's all over. Hey, if I thought it would work, then I'd already be on the floor giving it a go, but behaving like a loon isn't going to get me out of whatever this is, is it?

I follow him into the office and stop before I reach the desk. *"Wow."* I think to myself. Cruella's been keeping herself busy in here. It looks nothing like the office space that Graham used to vacate. Gone is his masculine, bare-minimal approach, instead, it's been completely transformed into what can only be described as an overindulgent hot, pink mess. Professor Umbridge would be so proud. Really the only thing that's missing is the cat wall plates.

Now, I'm quite a girly girl myself, but the amount of pink, in a wide variety of different shades is sickening. The upturned set of Graham's mouth shows me that he agrees with me too; one hundred percent. She's definitely gone all out on this little project. I wonder how much the company had to fork out for this little feng-shui project?

"So, do you want to start, or shall I?"

"Okay." I begin. Bloody hell, I've not been this nervous around him since the day he interviewed me. "Truthfully, I'm not sure what's going on here, but from the way that you're acting, I'm gonna take a wild guess and say it's quite serious?"

Graham lowers himself down into his old leather chair and flexes his fingers a little before entwining them together and then placing them upright on top of the desk. He doesn't answer me, so I take his silence as an affirmative yes. Instead, he raises his eyebrows slightly at me, silently asking me to continue.

"Honestly Graham, I'm so lost here. How about you help a girl out. Give me some kind of clue, please?"

"Sit." His voice comes out firm and he nods towards the chair opposite him, but I'm too scared to move, worried that if I do, he'll bark at me again. I really don't like the man that he's become since he's been away. It's been what, two weeks? I don't recognise any part of him right now. He used to be so full of compassion, fun, and love. He used to be a giggle a minute. No matter what, Graham always looked after his own. *"And they say you know a guy."* I think to myself. "You know, just because I'm not here every day, that doesn't mean that I don't know what's been going on, or what's been happening."

"Well, that's good to know," I say sarcastically "because like I said, I'm completely out of it here. So please, go ahead and enlighten me." I've been a solid, dedicated, hardworking and reliable employee at this firm for over five years now. To be fair, it's probably the most reliable thing in my life right now. Actually, it is the only reliable thing in my life. Wow, thinking about it like that, it's pretty depressing for an almost thirty-year-old. Not that I can do much about that right now. I'll just have to save it and weep later, preferably with a large glass of wine.

"Enlighten you, I shall. Sit, please." He says again. Now it could be me imagining it, but I'm pretty sure he almost choked on his manners just then. Unable to take the tension much longer, I pull out the chair and plonk my arse in it, wishing all this was over already.

"Okay Emily, look I like you, I've always liked you. You're a good asset to this company, which I'm sure that you'll more than agree." Err... that would be a mahoosive hell yes. I don't blow my own trumpet all that much, hardly ever actually, but one thing that I do know is that there's no denying that I'm shit hot when it comes to my job.

"But…" I add, almost certain where this conversation is heading but unable to hold my tongue. Plus, no matter the situation, there always seems to be a *but* in this life.

"But," he continues, painfully dragging this pointless situation on. Maybe he's after a dramatic effect or something? Well if he is, he's going the bloody right way about it. "Well, what can I say? These are words I never thought I'd have to say, least to you of all people." Graham takes a deep breath, and a look of pity sweeps across his mature face, making him look thoroughly stressed. From where I'm sitting, whatever he's trying to tell me, he clearly doesn't want to say it.

"For crying out loud Graham, just spit it out. I'm a big girl, I'm sure I can take it."

"I'll ask you one last time Emily, is there anything that you would like to tell me?"

"No, absolutely nothing. I don't know what you want me to do Graham. None of this is making any sense."

"Well then, I guess I'm afraid I'm left with no choice but to suspend you with immediate effect until further notice."

Wait, what? "Shut the front door," I say. This has got to be some kind of joke. "Suspend me?" I burst out laughing, unable to stop myself, but Graham's face doesn't falter. That man's poker face is on point, that's for sure. "Okay, okay, you got me. I bet everyone's in on it too, aren't they? Where'd you hide them? You may as well tell them to come out now." I look around the office, half expecting Matt and Cruella, maybe the other guys to come barrelling through the office door at any minute. What sick and twisted individuals do I spend most of my time around? Seriously, why would anyone want to pull a prank like that?

"Unfortunately, it's not a joke Emily."

"But... but it has to be. Why would you say that you were suspending me if it wasn't a joke? Come on Gray, you can't suspend me." He's got no grounds to suspend me on. This is bullshit.

"Emily, I think you'll find that I can and I am." He replies flatly.

"On what grounds? I haven't done anything to warrant this." Have I? I'm good at my job. I'm punctual, hardworking and I sure as hell wipe everyone else's arse. I love my job. I love the banter; everything that this place brings. "Are you feeling okay? I don't mean to be rude, but has it ever crossed your mind that you could potentially be on the verge of a mid-life crisis? Maybe a minor mental breakdown? I'm not saying it like it's a bad thing, these kind of things happen to people all the time." I've watched numerous shows to back this up too. "You might think that you're acting rationally now, but believe me, you're not. I've never seen him like this. Not once, in over five years. In my eye's he's being completely and utterly irrational here and he can't even see it. "Why don't you sleep on it?"

"Emily, it's out of my hands." I watch as he pulls his hand down over his gruff five o'clock shadow and I have to admit, he looks a little defeated. Deep down I can see that he really doesn't want to do this. Maybe there's still hope after all?

"So, it's really not some sick joke that you've decided to play on me? This is all happening?" The realisation of his previous words hit me; hard. Super hard, like one of those horrific kidney punches that catch you off guard. "Suspended?" I say again, more to myself, allowing it to register in my frazzled head.

"Gross misconduct is a serious issue, Emily. Like I said, it's all out of my hands now."

"How can it be out of your hands? You're the boss. The Don of this whole empire. The Tony Montana."

"I was." He says and the tiniest smile plays on his lips, but it's gone again in an instant. "That's now Amanda's role."

"What?" I blurt out before I can stop myself. I don't know why I'm so surprised, I should have seen this coming. I mean, what isn't Cruella in control of these days? She's well and truly stuck her fake claws in and taking poor Daddy dearest for everything that he's got. "Maybe I could…" I start begrudgingly, but Graham quickly cuts me off.

"While this investigation is taking place, you'll have no contact with Amanda, whatsoever. Is that understood?"

"But you just said she's my boss now?"

"Emily, please don't make this anymore difficult than it already is. I'm sorry, really I am, but you need to go and collect your belongings and I'm sure H.R will be in touch soon."

"This is unreal. I don't even know what it is that I'm supposed to have done. Is there an appeals process? Surely I've got rights too?"

"At this stage all I can say is that there have been some serious allegations concerning you that have been brought to my attention. These kinds of incidents can't be brushed under the carpet either, Emily. There are rules and regulations for a reason. I'm sure you understand, no?"

Hang on, he's suspending me and then asking me to understand? Talk about kicking me when I'm down. "No actually, no, I don't."

How does he expect me to understand? I arrived at work, bright eyed and bushy tailed just like any other Friday, only to be whipped into the office to be told that I'm being suspended for only God knows what. Surely any minute now I'll wake up and this will all me some crazy mind fuck that only my head can conjure. I place my hand on my thigh and pinch myself; hard.

Nope, nothing. I'm still sat here and this is still happening. *Shit.* "So, how long will all this take, then?" I ask, silently admitting defeat in my head. He's quite clearly not prepared to budge on this matter and whatever it is that has been brought to his attention, well, he's made his own personal judgment, hasn't he? Like he said, it's out of his hands, yadda, yadda.

"I can't give you a time frame Emily, you know that." He sighs.

"Just something? Surely you can give me that?" Anything, I don't care what, just something so I can tell that above everything else, he hasn't given up on me just yet.

"It could be a day, a week, maybe a month or more. I really don't know. I'm not trying to be awkward here Emily, really, I'm not. I just don't want to give you any false hope."

"A month? A whole month… or more?" I exclaim. "Graham, it's almost Christmas, and now I'm jobless." Freaking great. I suppose he doesn't need to worry about that, though, as it's not his life and career on the line. Oh God, I really don't want to go down the hooker route, but what choice is he actually giving me here?

"You're not jobless… yet. My hands are tied and I really shouldn't be involving myself in this investigation. It won't be good for anyone if that happens." He says very matter of fact. What's that even supposed to mean, if he gets involved? Isn't he already involved because he's my boss?

Where has the old Graham gone? The one that's facing me looks like a morbid shell of the old guy that I used to look up to. If that's what age does to you, then someone needs to find me some magic potion asap. I'd hate to grow old just to end up miserable and have the life sucked out of me.

"Right well, I guess that's that, then," I say, confirming the inevitable. As much as I want to, I can't meet his eyes. If I do, I know I'll only end up crying and ruining my perfect smoky eye and winged liner.

No one, I repeat, no one on this planet is worth that kind of sacrifice.

Chapter 9

I don't know what time it is. I don't even know how long ago my phone decided to turn against me too and die. What I do know is that it's cold. Oh, so cold. Possibly minus 20 right now. My nipples are painfully sore and my arse is shockingly numb. Even an Indian heatwave wouldn't warm me up quick enough.

I'm going to take a wild guess and say it's around 6 pm-ish. The sky's pitch black, the only visible light around is coming from the Christmas lights, magically flashing away in the distance. Only I don't feel all that magical anymore, not at all, and dare I say it, even Christmassy.

Today has well and truly killed off all of my Christmas spirit and I am not *that* person; ever. I'm always excited around Christmas time. Bloody hell, I still can't get to sleep on Christmas Eve. There's just way too much excitement, especially the big man's arrival. Yet right now I feel like Scrooge sat on this bench, waiting for the Ghost of Christmas past to come and haunt me.

I've been sat on this freezing cold park bench since I was wrongfully removed from the office. I can't say I've achieved much except mulling things over in my mind, trying to decipher what could have happened, what it is that I'm supposed to have done so wrong. But surprise, surprise, I'm coming up empty time and time again.

I know why I'm coming up empty, it's because I know that I've done nothing wrong, but would Graham listen to me? Would he heck. To be honest, I really can't believe how heartless Graham's been. Jesus, he could have waited until after Christmas to spring this kind of crap on me. Allowed me a couple of weeks before he took the plunge. He could have started his own little investigation instead of rushing straight to bloody H.R.

"Oh, what are you going to do, Parker?" My subconscious shouts out. He didn't even tell me if I'm going to get paid. Do you get paid whilst being suspended? It's never really been something that I've had to think about, to be honest. How in the name of everything holy am I going to survive? Yes, I'm exceptionally fortunate that I don't have rent or a mortgage to pay, but this chicks still got to eat. It's not like those tight-fisted sods at the bank will increase my credit card limit. I knew I should have kept it for emergencies, but it was just sitting so pretty and new in my purse. How could I not show it some love?

Sod this.

This is bloody ridiculous. I'm not putting up with this. I've put too much of my own time and energy into that place. If they expect me to go down without a fight, then they've got another thing coming, let me tell you. Both Cruella and H.R will be getting quite a mouthful from me in the morning. Who knows, maybe then they might just have something to suspend me for.

Gross misconduct, my arse. I have been and always will be a picture of pure professionalism. I reckon Judge Rinder would love to hear all about this little situation. Oh, I'd love to hear him shout and snap them right back into their place.

My phone's not been switched on all that long and already it's constantly buzzing around on the side. There must be a bazillion messages from Rachel and Matt. It's not stopped buzzing since it came back to life. I tried my best to ignore it and after five minutes I'd had enough and switched it onto silent with the vibration setting removed. I guess normal people would love to feel popular after the horrific day that I've just had, but to be fair, I really don't want to do normal right now. I really don't want to adult at all.

I grab a glass from my overly stocked cupboard and take a chilled bottle of wine from the fridge as I pass and take a seat at the kitchen table; alone, once again.

Maybe it's about time that I started to invest in some cats. I guess that's all I'll be good for these days. Boxsets, Vinnie, wine, and cats. I mean, I can't keep hold of the love of my life, I'm almost thirty and I'm fast becoming a Tinder trollop, and the best of it is, I managed to get myself removed from the one thing I'm actually good at and I haven't got the foggiest as to why.

I'm so ready for this year to be over already. It's been the shittiest one of my existence so far. Rachel's adamant that I've been on some amazing journey of discovery, but personally, I just think someone out there is playing evil, twisted mind games at my expense.

I never imagined that this is how my life would pan out. Me and Tyler had it all planned out. Holidays, marriage and kids. You name it, we planned for it. God, we were so happy, sickeningly so. Bloody hell, even I used to blush at the two of us together. We were both massive lovers of PDA's. Five years we were together. Five long, amazingly breath-taking years and we were inseparable. He was my everything, my Khal, my king and I truly believed that we were destined to grow old not so gracefully together. Fluffy ears and all. Him, not me, obviously. We used to laugh as we imagined what we'd be like as we queued up for our pensions. But, like everything else around me, it crumbled and fell to shit, big time.

It all started when Tyler got promoted at work. I was so happy and super proud of him. If ever anyone deserved the recognition, then it was Tyler. My very own life-sized action man was out there taking the business world by storm, just like he deserved. He was so happy too, at least for a while, anyway. Like a big fat pig in shit, but then gradually when the reality of his long hours kicked in, we started to see less of each other. Communication was now practically none existent between us, and even when I bit my lip and tried my best to talk to him, he'd just get really irritated and snap at me for no reason. He was a completely different person to the man that I knew and loved.

Bloody hell, it was hard. Watching the one person who means the most to you, slowly and painfully slipping out of your grasp and there's nothing that you can do about it. No matter how hard you fight, how hard you love. When they no longer care for you, no longer need you, they're gone.

"How'd your day go?" I'd ask him multiple times as soon as he stepped through the door after a busy day, hoping that eventually one night he'd wake up and realise what an absolute arse he was being and go back to normal. Our kind of normal.

Unfortunately, that day never arrived. Nine times out of ten, his dinner would be stone cold and dried up in the oven. The most that I would ever get back in response would be, "yeah, I'm beat. I'm gonna grab a shower and call it a night." Five years of constant love and affection and that's the response I got every single bloody time.

A wet splash lands on my hand, dragging me out of my painful memories. Memories that I've tried to shut out at every possible moment. *Oh, Emily, we can't be spilling precious wine, you silly girl. That's a bloody sin.*

It's only when a few more drops splatter, that I realise it's not wine at all, but my tears. I'm crying for God sake. Now it's all going down the pan. Crying for what was, or what could have been, I'm not too sure. Maybe it's a little bit of both. But, they say that you have to allow the tears to come so you can see things from a clearer view, or something like that.

"Give your bloody head a wobble, Parker. Your tears can't change the past." I mentally scold myself. I know that I shouldn't be wasting my energy on him, but I know that if he was here with me right now, then he'd know exactly what to do and he'd have all the magical words to make me feel better. Bloody selfish bastard. Why the hell did he have to go and break my heart?

The package that he sent me is still facing me, in its new-found resting place on the kitchen table. To be fair, what with all the hoo-hah today, I'd forgotten all about it for a little while. Now, however, looking right at it, in all its plain brown glory, it just feels like a harsh slap to the face. Reminding me once again what once was, or could have been.

"Should I open it?" I ponder out loud. When Mr. Jones passed it to me, I had no idea who it was from. Had things stayed that way, then I definitely would have opened it as soon as I stepped foot through the door.

I'm curious, deadly curious, but at the same time, I'm absolutely crapping it. If I'm being completely honest with myself and shake off this fake bravado that I've started to carry around with me, if I actually allowed myself to be truthful with my feelings, then I'd admit that my poor little heart is still fragile. What if when I open it, it rips my heart open all over again? All my hard work would have been for nothing.

My fingers reach out for it on impulse, hovering cautiously, my whole body riddled with nerves. I almost touch the box, but my hand whips back again just as the front door knocks, breaking the deathly silence that's currently encasing my house.

Maybe I could pretend that I'm not home? For all anyone knows, I could have been whipped off my feet by some handsome prince who's only purpose in life is to make me happy and force me to forget my old, shit excuse of a life.

I should be so bloody lucky.

The knock sounds again, more persistent this time. "Oh, just piss off and leave a girl alone. I don't want to donate to anything right now and I most certainly don't want to be stood out in the cold making pointless small talk." I huff out loud and mutter into my wine glass as if this magical potion completely understands and has answers for me.

Knock… Knock… Knock…

Well, whoever it is, it doesn't sound like they're planning to leave anytime soon. Oh crap, what if it's Mr. Jones? Maybe I should go and check. Thinking back, I've not heard him all night since I've been back, which is pretty strange for your average Friday night. Normally anyone would think that I lived next door to some rowdy teenagers who've just found their freedom, not an old aged pensioner.

I reluctantly pull myself away from my pity party for one and head towards the front door, albeit a little wobbly on my feet from my wine consumption. One of these days I will learn to eat something before I drink.

"Parker, open up. I know that you're in there." Great, this is all I need. "I'm not leaving until you answer. I'll happily freeze my balls off all night if I have too."

As tempting as that sounds, I just don't have the heart to do it. I'd hate for anyone to suffer. Well, everyone except Graham the grumpy fucking goose. What a wanker.

I take one last step towards the door, resting my hand on the door handle and I take a deep breath, ready to plaster on my show stopping fake smile and swing the door open; already fully aware who's on the other side.

"About bloody time." Matt cries out, just as an icy cold gust of wind whips past me. He's alright, though. He looks all snug and warm in his thick wooly scarf and black trench coat. I can just about make out his rosy red cheeks, mostly hidden from his dark, gruff stubble. The contrast doesn't half make his lips look deeper and fuller, causing his green eyes to sparkle brightly. Wow. I have to admit that if I didn't know him already, he'd definitely make my head turn, that's for sure. "I've brought wine."

"Come on in, then," I say swiftly, the cold attacking me from every possible angle, in turn causing me to shiver unpleasantly.

"You lost your phone? I've been calling you all day." He says, a scolding tone in his voice is evident but right now I can't be arsed retaliating. I watch as he wastes no time in removing his scarf and coat, revealing a very complimentary muscle hugging grey, charcoal jumper. Well, you can't miss his bloody biceps in that, that's for sure. Not that these eyes of mine are complaining or anything.

"I've been…" I pause, searching for the right words to explain my crapper of a day. "busy." Well, it's not a huge lie, just a teeny, tiny white one. I have been super busy with my thoughts. "Not to be rude Matt, but, why are you here?"

His emerald eyes meet mine and he looks at me like I've lost my mind. "I wanted to come and see you after today, you know?" He hops from one foot to another, shaking the bottle of wine back and forth in his hands.

"Should we be celebrating something?" I ask, confused as hell. Why would we be celebrating anything?

"I thought you'd want a drink, after…" Matt continues. I roll my eyes, spin on my heels and head back to my pity party. No sooner have I reached the table, fully intending to plonk my backside back down into my chair for the foreseeable, it hits me. Bam, right in the freaking face. I don't sit down, instead, I spin right around to face him. "Oh. My. God... Did you know? You knew and you didn't even tell me? How could you not have the decency to at least warn me before I headed to the office?"

"Erm... yeah." He replies cautiously, fully aware that he has awoken the inner bitch. Everyone knows once she's out, it's a hard task getting her back in that box. Even I struggle and she's my pissing bitch.

"Well... Why didn't you at least give me a heads up?" I snap.

"Whoa Parker, calm down a little. I did. I emailed you last night. Around 8-ish. I thought you knew, that's why I texted you good luck this morning."

I'd like to believe that he's telling me the truth, but I don't know what to believe anymore. It feels like everyone I let in does nothing but shit on me time and time again. "Well, I didn't receive any emails from you. Where'd you send it?" I ask, hoping to catch him out. God, maybe that's not such a good idea seeing as though my phone's shocking. It's less than a month old and I've had nothing but problems with it and that was before the screen shattered. But, it's an iPhone. The apple whore inside me refuses to believe that it's the phone. Obviously, it is, but right now I'll happily blame google and my internet provider, or anyone else for that matter. Just not Apple.

To be fair, though, I can't even remember if I even bothered to check them last night. My head was way too muddled with images of my Thor like creature of a date to even contemplate carrying out the most mundane of tasks.

"Personal and work." Matt muffles while pouring himself a glass of wine and topping mine up as he goes. "I wasn't sure which one you'd check first so thought it would be best to go for both."

"Are you sure? " I ask him. I grab my phone from the side and open my emails, which takes me a while with the shattered screen. Fortunately I know the phone like the back of my hand. Sure enough, there's his email. I click on it so that I can read what he's put and I can just about make it out.

Good luck tomorrow, Parker. You're sure going to need it. Call me the minute you leave the office. Are we clear?

"Well, I've got this one. I didn't get the one at work, though. I briefly checked them this morning. Maybe you thought you'd sent it to that one? Anyway, regardless; you knew. I didn't and that email doesn't exactly prepare me for much, does it? I still haven't got a clue what it's all about, to be honest."

"Well, there wasn't that much to tell really. I didn't want to jinx you or put my foot in it, you know? All I knew was that Graham sent an email around yesterday informing us that as a bonus for all our hard work we could have the day off. An early Christmas present, apparently. I went to reply to you to see if you fancied doing something, but then I saw that you weren't on the list. It was all a little too fishy if you ask me. I knew that there could only be one reason why Graham would want you in that office." He smiles and takes a glug of wine before continuing. "Well, come on. Don't keep me hanging like a pair of Bridget's, Parker. I want to know; did it happen, or not?"

Considering Matt knew all about today, he's acting pretty happy about it all. "What about Cruella? I take it she was in on all this too? You've become quite the pair, haven't you?" No doubt he's probably shagging her too. "Her, I can understand, but you? I thought that we were a team, Matt? I thought we were friends? Listen," I whisper, hoping that will prevent my voice from breaking. "I'd be lying through my teeth if I said I wasn't upset today, but you've just well and truly kicked me in the balls." I really want to grab my drink, God knows I need it, but it's on the table right next to Matt's big, strong arms and I know that if I take one step closer to him, I'll end up going for him and it won't end well at all. How could he do this to me? We're married in the workplace for God sake. He's supposed to have my back and I have his. Those were our unspoken vows. Till P45's do us part.

"Why would you be upset?" He asks. "I brought some wine to help you celebrate." He looks utterly confused and I almost begin to feel sorry for him. Almost.

"Are you taking the piss? Why would I be celebrating? Fucking hell Matthew, do you even know what happened today? And before you answer, I'd think long and hard about it." My voice cracks. That's it, gone. All my composure that I've been trying to hold together is slipping bit by bit and I'm really struggling to keep all my anger, hurt and frustration locked away. So far, I'm not doing so well and any minute now, this bitch is going to blow.

"You finally got promoted?" He asks, a little bit of hope shines through his voice.

My eyes fly back towards Matt and I stare him down. Is this all some sick joke to him? "Say, what now? Why on God's green earth would you think that I would get promoted? Try suspended."

Chapter 10

It turns out that Matt was just as oblivious to my new-found suspension as I was. At least he's still rooting for team Emily, then. I suppose I should be happy that the boy knows exactly where his loyalties should lie, but I'd still bet my life that he'd poke that horrific demon, Cruella given half the chance. That is if he hasn't done so already.

"I'll grab another bottle." I slur, quietly eyeing the three empty bottles that are currently occupying my kitchen table. I know that I'm going to suffer like a MoFo tomorrow, but right now I really couldn't give a toss about it. Any of it. Well, it's not like I've got anything to get up for anymore, is it? I could become a raving lush, more so than I am now and be guilt free while binging on the latest box sets.

"You know, all this has to be some kind of sick and twisted messed up joke. No way would Graham suspend you. It's just not his style." Matt chimes in as I carefully and not too soberly step back towards out little party for two. You know, I wasn't all that keen on these black and white tiles for the kitchen floor originally, but by God have they saved me from breaking my neck on multiple occasions. So longs as I remember to look down and step perfectly over them, I usually remain vertically upright. Good old Gran, watching out for me once again. Plus, there's no denying that they'd make a cracking board for a real-life game of wizard's chess.

"Exactly," I say. "I don't know how many times I asked him as to why, either. He definitely wasn't ready for playing ball and giving me an answer. Apparently, in his words, it's best for everyone if he doesn't get involved." I shrug, utterly defeated. The only thing left to do is grab my wine glass and take a massive glug of the good stuff.

"Bollocks. That's bullshit Parker and you know it. They have to tell you the reason for the suspension. Unless..." Matt's eyes drop down to the table and he falls unusually quiet. Now is not the time for bloody quiet.

"Unless what?" I shout, demanding answers.

"Unless. I don't know, maybe the company's struggling and Graham's suspended you while he decides if he really needs to lay you off?"

"No, it can't be that. If I was being laid off I'd like to think that he'd at least have the decency to tell me the script right from the off."

"What, like he's been up front and honest with you today?"

I decide it's probably best to ignore Matt's little comment. I don't think I need to be reminded of what went down earlier. "Plus, I'd also like to think that you'd be having the same conversation with him too if that's the case."

"I guess you're right."

"He just wasn't himself, though." I add. "He was all hard and cold, nothing like the big soft teddy bear that we all know and love."

"That's business, sweetheart. I wouldn't take it personally." Matt sing songs and I know that he's just trying his best to cheer me up, but it's not working.

"No?" I reply sarcastically. "I love you Matthew, but you ain't half full of shit at times." Dick. It's all right for him to sit here and say that, he's not the bloody one in the firing line, is he? No, that would be yours truly.

My head's going to be so bad tomorrow. I'm trying my best to focus and listen to what Matt's jabbering on about, but it's all white noise. It really doesn't help matters that when I look up at him all I can see is two of him swaying back at me. Truthfully, this is fast becoming quite the habit.

"Hmm?" I say, silently praying that I've chimed in at the right minute. One look at him and his wide green eyes show me that I haven't. Shoot.

"You do, huh?" He slurs back at me. Shit, I better start listening to what he's saying to me, otherwise, I could end up in all kinds of trouble.

"I do, what? Sorry, you lost me for a second there."

"Thought as much." He laughs back at me and it's such a happy, carefree laugh. Oh, I've always been quite fond of his laugh. "I said I'm well smashed. Do you want me to stay over?"

"Thanks, but I'll be fine, I'm a big girl, you know. I'll probably just crash out in a minute anyway." Right after I've been sick, but I'm sure he'll live a much more satisfactory life without knowing that teeny, tiny piece of information. I look down towards my empty glass sitting innocently on the table and begin to debate whether or not I should have anymore. My little red devil on my shoulder is all for it, dancing up and down excitedly, pressing its hot fork into my skin shouting, *"Oh, go on. Just one more drink..."*

"Right Parker, if it's all right with you then, I'm gonna shoot."

At the sound of those words, my mind automatically wanders off to me being all tucked up in bed, nice and cosy with nothing but four spinning walls for company and it sounds like sheer bliss.

Tiredness suddenly consumes every inch of me and I feel like I could sleep for all eternity. Well, there's not really much stopping me, is there? Yes, bed is a bloody good idea, probably the best one that I've had all day. I lift my heavy eyes from my glass and I try my best to focus on Matt...

Wow. What the actual fuck?

Nothing in this world and absolutely no amount of alcohol could have ever prepared me for this. How the hell did this happen? How did I get from trying to listen to Matt as best as I could to... this? I'm unable to move, my whole body is rigid, completely routed to the spot from shock?

Matt's manly scent dangerously mixed with alcohol and the faded smell of Boss original totally consume me and take over all my senses as his lips gently trace mine. Any rational thoughts that I may have had, have long gone, packed their bags and left for the hills. They've upped sticks; just like that, without any bloody care as to how I'm supposed to cope in this situation.

This is wrong. I know it's wrong, but dear God it also feels oh, so, right. I'm feeling places of my body that I never even knew existed, and some that have been dormant for far too long.

All too soon, Matt pulls away from me, his right hand delicately encasing my face as he says, "are you all right?"

I don't answer him straight away. My body is defying me here at every possible turn. Jesus Christ, I'm wasted and my head's already over the place without throwing this little game changer into the mix. My lips feel cold and bare at the sudden loss of contact with him and I'm not too sure how I feel about it. Strange, yes. Completely taken aback, abso-fricking-lutely. My head starts to spin again, yet I don't remember it spinning while Matt was kissing me. Oh, I really don't want it to spin anymore. Without giving it too much thought, I find myself launching all 9 stone 10 of me directly at him, not really giving two hoots as to whether I'm acting like a raving sex deprived hussy, because, well come on let's face it, I am. I can't really deny it, and I've been celibate for an absolute age.

"Easy, tiger." Matt gently mouths against my lips as I almost send us both toppling backwards onto the kitchen floor from my new found drunken strength. "*Hulk doesn't have shit on me.*" I silently giggle to myself.

"Shhh…" I reply out loud, before staking my claim on him and grabbing a firm hold of those perfectly, beautiful, manly and sinful biceps. "Don't talk, just kiss me." I demand and God love him, he's happy to oblige.

Although I'm having a right whale of a time now, I just hope that my sober mind doesn't live to regret this. The self-doubt in the back of my mind is currently dancing proudly with her pom-poms letting me know that regret is well and truly on the cards, so I shut her out, locking her into the back of my head while I enjoy the feeling of this manly beast before me.

My breathing is still taking over my body and my chest rises and falls rapidly and I'm struggling to control it.

WOW…

Just wow. I don't really have any other words to describe what just happened. Did I dream it? No, that's not possible, it was far too real and too good to be just a dream. I look to my right and see Matt's muscular back on display with one of his long, lean legs sprawled out on top of the quilts. Funnily enough, I must admit that I kind of like the look of him sprawled out completely naked on my bed. I could stare at his body all day long, well, at least when he doesn't know that I'm doing it. Trust me, Matt really doesn't need any form of ego boost.

One thing I do hate though, is snoring. I hate it with an absolute passion. So much so that I often thought of murdering Tyler because of it. There's nothing worse than broken sleep. I soon came to realise why people are known to use it as a form of torture. Shitting hell, deny me of my sleep and I'll tell you everything. Scrap that, I'd even go as far to tell you what you actually wanted to hear, whether it's the truth or not, just so I could drift back off to dreamland.

I don't have a clue how I'm going to cope if I ever decide to have kids. Maybe I'll need to get a nanny. Yes, a nanny is a must. I'll be no bloody good to them wandering around zombified would I?

I don't think I really need to worry about the possibility of kids anytime soon though, I kind of don't have the other half of the required body parts around to make that stuff happen. Right now though, I think that's the least of my worries.

The one thing that I should be focusing on is what I'm going to say to Matt when he wakes up. Did I regret it? No, not really. Will I feel awkward when I have to face him? One hundred percent, but we're both adults so hopefully it will be as pain free as possible, said no one; ever.

Chapter 11

Melody Grace is my friend. Of course, for all intents and purposes, the girl sat before me is also my work colleague, but firstly and most importantly, she's my friend.

I don't know why she still holds that title personally, considering she's only just got back from sunning herself in Dubai. Little old me, jealous? Not much. Well, tans are so overrated these days. People are crying out for pale, milk bottle coloured skin, dusted with a few freckles here and there. Freckles really get the pasty look on point. At least that's what I've always told myself, anyway.

Do you know that you can now buy transfer freckles for your day to day look? I shit you not, it's true. All this time I've tried to change my look by caking my foundation on when I was a teenager, and now people want to be pale faces. I give up. Honestly, I do.

I guess the saying is true; you always want what you don't have.

I knew that I'd see her once she arrived back home eventually, because, well, that's what friends do. What I didn't expect was to be spending my Monday morning with her at *'Rachel's Place'*, that's for sure.

"Mel, you know that you shouldn't be here," Rachel whispers disapprovingly as she carefully hands out our lattes. Oh, here we go. She's always been a swot when it comes to punctuality and conduct. I could never work for her. Actually, scrap that. One day I might be left without much of a choice, but I'd bloody hate every single second of it, I just know it.

"Well, I'm not moving so you may as well fill that hole of yours with a muffin or something if you can't be quiet." Dear God. I love them both, really, I do, but they don't half clash. I guess it's because they're too much alike get along or see eye to eye, but no matter what, they're always here for me when I need them the most.

"She's right, you know," I say quietly, whilst being a coward and hiding behind my overly large cup. Yes, I'm a wimp and proud. Mel can be a little hasty at times and I don't fancy wearing her latte anytime soon. Plus, this Lipsy dress wasn't cheap. Usually I'd wait until the sales started, but I needed to have it there and then. That's when me and Mr Plastic were good friends, happily splashing the cash during our honeymoon period. I remember it well.

"Don't you bloody start," she warns and gives me one of her certified glaring looks. "I'm here and I'm not moving until something changes. End of. Call it a strike if that makes you feel any better, but us girls have to stick together."

"Mel..." Both Rachel and I say in unison.

"It's not important. It'll all be fine, you'll see."

"But..." I try my best to continue, but she slams her latte glass down in the most diva-like fashion, even Mariah would be scared for her crown in this moment.

"Listen to me Emily, as soon as Matt called I knew something was up. Matt never calls anyone; like ever. Too much of a snapchatter, that one, but what can you do? After I'd spoken to him, I knew where I needed to be and that's right here, with you." Melody looks at me and then she rolls her eyes towards Rachel's direction. She silences her with one look as soon as Rachel tries to argue back. God, I really wish that one day I'll be able to master that skill. To be honest though, I'd much rather be hashing it out with George right now, instead of being stuck in the middle of these two.

"What exactly did Matt say to you?" I ask nervously and begin to fiddle with the corners of the menu on the table. It's the one question that's been hanging on my tongue since the second she mentioned his name and now it's bloody slipped out before I could stop it.

"Matt?" Oh my God, holy mother of Jesus. Palpitations begin to hammer in my chest at the mere mention of his name and cold, sticky sweat starts to coat my palms as I wait for Mel to answer me. Why isn't she answering me?

Oh, God. He's told her, hasn't he? He's only gone and opened that big, fat trap of his. I'm going to kill him when I see him. Maybe that won't be so easy after all. Luckily for him, I don't have to face him today, or any day for the foreseeable, when I come to think about it.

"Well?" I ask, hoping to get some kind of answer out of her. I'm bloody going out of my mind here. I spot Rachel eyeing me suspiciously from her seat to my right, her lips pressed into a perfect pout, trying her best to figure out why I'm so keen to know. Well, if they didn't already know by now that I slut dropped him, they sure as bloody hell do now.

I haven't mentioned Friday night to anyone. Not Rachel, not Mel, I've not even really admitted it out loud to myself. Sooner or later I know that I'm going to have to admit it, I know, but right now I'd rather forget. After all, it's not like he's tried to check in on me since. Not even one lousy snapchat.

The bastard.

To be fair, he didn't really say much to me before he left either. I offered him a coffee to which he politely declined, gave me an awkward and pretty much forced kiss on the cheek and went on his merrily little way, not even bothering to turn back once.

"Nothing all that exciting really. Come on, it's Matt. The most exciting he gets is a Gregg's for lunch on a Wednesday." I think I can beg to differ on that front. But, there's no reason for me to bring that to their attention. "To be fair, I switched off to his ramblings as soon as he said suspension. You know, I bet Amanda's got something to do with this."

And this is why we are friends. We think exactly the same, yet I'm the one to actually sit back and try my best to evaluate the situation instead of running in all guns blazing, unlike this one.

"You know, I won't lie to you. That did kind of cross my mind too, but something like that would be too easy for her and plus, what's she really got to gain from seeing me off, really?" Cruella kept going through my head over and over while I was freezing my arse off on that shitty little park bench, but as easy as it could be to point the finger at her, it just doesn't seem right. Okay, there's no denying that we don't like each other and we only talk when we have to, so why would she want me out? "She'd be right up shit street if that's the case. Now that I'm not there, wiping everyone's arses, all the figures that I've kept above board are going to drop quicker than her knickers on a Friday night."

"That's true. Maybe she sees you as some kind of threat? Either way, it's got dodgy as shit written all over it. I've got a bloody mind to email Graham directly and see what the hell he thinks he's playing at. And to think I always thought he was a decent guy…"

"Good luck with that." Rachel pipes up complete with a little miss know it all expression firmly fixed on her face. "What? You know being AWOL is probably one of the biggest forms of gross misconduct that there is, don't you? I highly doubt they'd suspend you, more like you'd be sacked on the spot."

"Rachel love, if I want your opinion I'll ask for it. Right now, I need your coffee's so snap to it."

"Mel," I say disapprovingly. I know the pair of them love to bicker, but she's going way too below the belt for my liking today.

"Oh, she knows that I love her really." She smiles with a dismissive wave of her hand and rolls her eyes at Rachel again. "I'm just trying to get my head around this whole situation."

"Yep, and I love you too. So much so, one of these days I might just lace your coffee with a teeny, tiny bit of arsenic."

"Mwah." Mel shoots her a kiss and I really want to smash their bloody stupid heads together.

"Pack it in girls. You're really not helping matters." I thought they were supposed to be here to support me, not to frigging point-score against one another.

"No? Maybe he will." I look at Rachel as her eyes grow wide and a humongous grin takes over her whole face. Oh, I know that look. I've witnessed it plenty of times before. It's a look that says 'oh boy are you in for it now.'

I don't even need to look behind me to know exactly who's stood a few feet behind me. Bloody hell, I can sense him and I can even smell him too. Every single hair on my body is raised and on edge, tingling with need and anticipation of what might happen.

And then my stomach drops. I look like shit. Absolute cow-turd. All I wanted to do this morning was vacate my personal pity party, get some fresh air and some adult, well, let's just say conversation for argument's sake, nobody likes to get all political, do they? So, up I got and off I popped to Rachel's, only to find Mel already waiting for me with a concerned expression on her face, yet laden with a bunch of holiday memorabilia.

For fuck sake. Why is this happening to me now? I haven't even brushed my hair and I don't have a single ounce of make-up on my pale and delicate looking skin. At just the thought of how dreadful I must look, my hands automatically reach out for the scraggily ends of my shaggy bob and I silently pray to everything that's holy that my waves pass off as sexy and not screaming lazy, trampy bitch, which in all honesty is what I really am.

"Holy mother of..."

"Melody," Rachel says sternly, abruptly stopping anything unladylike escaping her mouth.

"Who. Is. That?" Mel asks and her mouth is hanging open and she doesn't even have the decency to hide it, either. She's got zero shame as she practically drools over my very own Thor.

"Ladies." He croons, his voice deliciously deep and sending a multitude of shivers running through my body as he walks straight towards our table. I catch a glimpse of him and my God, he's just perfection. I've never known anything like it.

"But, what about Matt?" my nasty little devil decides to pipe up and remind me of my dirty and slutty ways.

"What about him?" I silently argue back.

"You weren't thinking too much about Noah while you were shagging the shit out of Matt, were you?"

"I'm single you little shit. I can do who and what the hell I want, when I want."

"So, we can see. I guess It looks like someone's really making up for lost time, aren't they?" He continues, trying to goad me further.

"Oh, piss off." I argue back again, trying to defend my silly, reckless actions. I can't believe that I'm arguing with myself over a man and a bloody penis of all things. When the hell did my life become so complicated?

"Hi." Mel swoons, a flirtatious tone very evident, bringing me right back to the here and now. I watch, slightly amused as he smiles politely at her, and then almost instantly his eyes fix themselves firmly back on mine and my poor heart does a little flutter.

"Emily." He nods and I bite down on my bottom lip, absolutely certain that my cheeks are now a lovely deep shade of crimson. As much as I'd love to reply back to him, the words just won't come and all I can muster is a goofy half smile.

Way to go, Parker.

As Noah makes his way towards the counter, Melody elbows me sharply in the side. "Ow. What the bloody hell was that for?" I scowl, gripping my side to try and stop the pain.

"Like you really need to ask? What was that?"

"What?" I'm trying my best to play dumb, but I already know that she's not going to have any of it. She wants answers. She's like a flaming vulture when she wants something, this one. There's just no stopping her.

"That. You. Him? I've only been away for a week and so far you've been suspended and now you've got some seriously hot as fuck business guy leering all over you."

"Oh, give over. You make it sound so much more dramatic than it actually is. Also, he wasn't leering, he was just being polite."

"Polite my arse. Anyway, I thought you were supposed to be crap at all this dating malarkey?"

"I am." I shout out in disbelief, while holding my hands up to show my innocence. "You should have seen the weirdo who I ended up with last week. Absolute fruit loop, he was." I'll never, ever forget how he's scared me for life. To be fair, since him I haven't looked at my own nipples the same. "Plus, to make things even more interesting, bloody Rachel's only gone and set me up on Tinder, hasn't she? Honestly, Mel, I can't even. I mean, I'm sure most of them have to be fake."

Some people on there really are destined to be single for all eternity, yet others have either nabbed some innocent soul's picture from google or they're clearly cheating on their poor, innocent wives, or girlfriends because looking like that, there's no frigging way that they can be single.

"Oh, please tell me you haven't. Bloody hell, Emily. I go away for a week..." She sighs disapprovingly at me.

"I'm only curious, plus it's a laugh that I could really do with right now." I watch her closely, but she still eyes me disapprovingly." Oh, come on, it's not like I'm gonna meet someone on there and we're going to run off into the sunset and live happily ever after, is it? You've got to think logical here, Mel."

"Well, I guess it's worked for some people. I just don't like it, personally it's not for me. You could end up with a right weirdo, or psycho. But, then again, if you could meet someone like that," she swoops her head over towards Noah's direction again and I smile knowing exactly where her mind has wandered off too, "well, in that case, I'd be all for it."

I can't help but laugh at her, she's so bloody old fashioned at times. "Well, I didn't stumble across him on Tinder. In actual fact, Rachel set me up with him on a blind date."

And with that, for what feels like the hundredth time this morning, Melody's jaw hits the floor and I feel a little smug on the inside. I just love what this girl does to my ego.

Chapter 12

I say my goodbyes to Rachel and Mel reluctantly, but I've got my routine smear appointment due in an hour and if I don't leave now, then I never will and being the good girl that I am, it's not something that I really want to miss and put to chance.

"I'll call you later," Rachel says as she pulls me into a tight embrace and I breathe in the familiar scent of DKNY. I don't know if it's Rachel, or the familiar scent, but it instantly puts me at ease and makes me feel right at home. My very own human comfort blanket.

"Me too." Mel agrees. "But first I'm going to head to the office to see what I can find out. That bitch better hope she doesn't bump into me, especially today of all days. She's got a lot to answer for, that much I am sure of."

"Is that really a wise move? You've been absent all morning."

"Jetlag. What can they do, really?" She shrugs. Nothing ever phases that woman at all. Sometimes I wish I could be more like her.

"Oh, Emily before you go, Noah asked me to give you this." I look around for him briefly and he's nowhere to be seen. How did I not see him leave? Great, I bet he's no longer interested in me now because I resemble a wild, feral drowned animal. Way to go, Parker, you're really doing a fantastic job today, aren't you?

"Well, you've obviously left some kind of impression on him." Rachel teases.

Obviously. Not.

I look down as Rachel places a rectangular box into my hand. I haven't got a clue what it could be, but the deep charcoal wrapping paper feels very rich and thick under my touch.

"Looks like you've got a thing for packages this week, girl." I inwardly groan as I'm suddenly reminded once again of the un-opened package on my kitchen table, courtesy of Tyler. Tyler the twat.

"Rach…" I warn.

"Don't worry about it now." She says empathetically and with that I squeeze her a little bit tighter. Mel doesn't need to know about it, not yet anyway. I'd never get out of here if that happens. Mel would have me marching back to my house just to grab it so that she can see what's inside. Actually, I'd probably go as far to say that she'd open it herself; with or without my permission.

"Right, girls," I say again as I look at the time on my beautiful apple watch. "I'm really going to have to love you and leave you." I give both of my friends one last kiss and dart out of the door, with Noah's gift firmly clenched in my hands.

"Miss Parker, please."

My vajayjay squeezes in protest. Who needs to do pelvic floor excercises when this is the reaction you get at the thought of a horrific plastic scope being shoved up you. There isn't any amount of lube that will ever make it comfortable. A violation, that's what it is.

I know that I need to have it done, that it's only five minutes of discomfort and being degraded is completely worth it when you look at the bigger picture, but by heck, it doesn't make it any easier.

You know you've hit a bloody bad patch when you shave especially for the doctor's office. Ugh, I'm really not looking forward to this at all. Yes, I know that they see foofs all the time, but not mine. Actually, putting aside my recent behaviour, I'm usually quite selective when comes to who sees my lady garden.

"Oh, you weren't that selective with Matt."

Brilliant, once again the devil has decided to rear his ugly frigging horns.

I don't even know what I'm supposed to do about this whole Matt situation. Bloody hell, it shouldn't even be a situation. But, it is and there's not much that I can do about it. Should I call him? What would I even say? *"Oh, hey. Thanks for a rocking time, how about we just get on with life and pretend like it never happened?"*

I don't want it to be awkward between us the next time that I see him. Saying that he's already acting like nothing's happened anyway as I've not heard from him at all over the weekend. Usually, he'd send something, or give the odd poke. Yes, Matt still pokes people. Why I'll never know, but it's true. I'm sure he must be the only person that still uses that feature on Facebook.

I guess the bottom line is that I mustn't be up there with his high standards of a shag. I'd love to say the same about him, but it was pretty enjoyable, to be fair. Whether that's because of how long I've gone without sex or not, I'll never know. But it was pretty much rather enjoyable all the same.

No more than fifteen minutes later, I'm in, scraped and back out again, all my dignity well and truly out of the window. Well, what I had left of it anyway, which was hardly any after this past weekend's reckless antics.

I nod my head to Sandra, my Mum's best friend and head medical secretary of our Doctor's practice as I leave. At least I can rest easy with the knowledge that within the next ten minutes or so Sandra will be straight on the blower to my Mum telling her just how much of a good girl I've been. Patient confidentiality doesn't really stretch all that far between those two, especially when it comes to things like routine smears. In all honesty, I don't think it stretches all that far between the two of them anyway. Thank God, I've never had any embarrassing sexual complaints. Jesus Christ, if I did then there's no way that I'd ever hear the end of it. Plus, I like to live my life just happily plodding along, safe in the knowledge that my Mamma still believes me to be one hundred percent virginal and completely untarnished.

To be fair, it was getting pretty close where I could have applied to be one of those rogue Nun's if I'd have gone without the good stuff any longer. Vinnie's a trooper and all, but there's just something about a hot solid piece of man-meat that really gets the blood pumping.

Just like that, Matt creeps into my mind again. No matter what I do, I just can't seem to shift him out of my head for long. Maybe me and alcohol shouldn't be friends. It's such a bad influence on me, always egging me on to make the wrong choices in life. Making me think that it's an amazing idea at the time, only for me to realise the next day that none of it was really the best option.

Seriously, what am I going to do about this whole Matt situation? I knew the whole thing was a bloody bad idea. Every single fiber of my being was telling me that something like this would happen. I guess it's fair to say that I've been living a lie for the past twenty-nine years. Ladies be warned, it's not just men that think and act with their Genitalia. Us girls and our vajayjay's are pretty rebellious too.

I know that it's not big and it's definitely not clever, I mean come on, just look where my carefree and reckless behaviour has gotten me so far, and I've not even been doing it all that long. I'll tell you where, absolutely nowhere, except feeling like a used piece of meat and that's not a nice feeling at all.

My phone buzzes to life in the back pocket of my jeans causing me to jump right out of my thoughts and straight into the back of a rather large and stocky guy.

"Sorry." I mouth quietly while my head faces down towards my flats.

"Hey, I know you?" He questions with certainty, yet his voice doesn't sound all that familiar.

I look up and take in the man stood before me and I can honestly say, hand on heart that I haven't got the foggiest idea as to who he is. "Nope, I'm sorry. I don't think you do." I reply as politely as possible while trying to wrack my brains. Surely, I'd remember the guy if I knew him?

"It's Emily, right?"

"Uh-huh." I reluctantly nod my head and feel like I'm auditioning for the part of Winston the dog in those bloody car insurance adverts. I'd probably pass as a good nodding dog with the way I feel right now. I'm totally confused and this stranger is watching me expectantly, patiently waiting for a big fat light to flash behind my eyes as the recognition kicks in. Well, I'm afraid he's going to be stood here for a ridiculously long time if that's the case.

"Are you trying to be funny? It's me, Scott?" He continues and I can't help but detect a teeny, tiny hint of desperation in his voice. "Scott-Scott…"

Pursing my lips together tightly, I try my best to think long and hard as to whether our paths have ever crossed before, but again I'm coming up blank. To tell you the truth, I'm pretty weirded out that he knows my name. That right there should be sounding all kinds of alarm bells. "Well, Scott-Scott, I'm really sorry to say that I don't have a clue who you are," I say apologetically and a tiny part of me feels a little bit gutted for the guy. He looks just like I felt when I found out that Santa wasn't real and it utterly destroyed me to know that it was really my Mum throwing back all the mince pies. I don't know how she hid all those bloody calories, either. Clearly, I didn't get those happy genes or her magical super powers.

All too quickly his whole posture changes before me. Gone is his warm happy smile, instead, it's replaced by a sharp and ferocious scowl and his body is all hard and ridged and I feel scared, which isn't something that I have ever felt outside in broad daylight since I was a little girl.

I really want to put one foot in front of the other, to get away from this weirdo, but then at the same time I can't help but feel rude. God knows why, I was as happy as happy can be walking down Oxford street, ready to grab a bite to eat from Marks' before heading back home to enjoy the rest of my day being a jobless and lonely old bum. But then again, I guess nothing is ever plain sailing, though, is it?

Now I've got this guy invading my dancing space and I don't like it one bit. For the love of God, he doesn't seem to take the hint. Johnny Castle would not approve of this *Scott-Scott's* attitude, let me tell you. I bet he'd be just the type to stick baby in the corner too.

See, this is how I know that I don't know this guy. There's no way on earth that I would ever be able to associate with people like that. My Mamma definitely didn't raise no fool, or whatever it is that they say.

All too suddenly, his left hand moves at super, fast speed and reaches inside his jacket pocket at the right hand side. *"Oh shit."* I've watched movies and everyone knows that there's only one thing that's hidden inside there, like ever. Death is coming for me and there's nothing that I can do about it. I'm well and truly screwed.

Has someone hired a hit-man out on me? It'd make bloody sense, wouldn't it? Random guy approaches an innocent young girl on the street and just so happens to know everything that there is to know about her. Said random guy then tries to leer innocent, young girl in and then... Boom. Gone, just like that. Never to be seen or heard from again.

Maybe if I cried out for help, made a couple of pleaful screams here and there, cause some kind of scene, maybe it would scare him just enough to back off. Hmm, or maybe that's what he'd expect me to do. I guess he must be some kind of professional, after all.

Realising that my fate now rests in Scott-Scott's hands, I take in a deep, long and what's most likely going to be my final breath and silently pray that it's all done as quickly and as pain-free as possible. No one really likes an overly dramatic victim at the best of times, and I don't think my fellow passers-by would feel any differently.

"Look..." He snaps at me, yet my eyes remain firmly fixed on my Primarni specials. Now, they might be the cheapest pair of shoes that I've ever purchased but by heck, they're definitely the most comfiest. To be fair, I half expected them to fall apart a long time ago, but no;

these little beauties are holding on nice and strong, the set of troopers that they are.

"I said look at me, Emily." A chill runs right down my spine at the sound of my name leaving his mouth and not in a good way. Not only is this guy seriously deluded, but it seems he's also a sadistic sod too. Why else would he want me to look him in the eye just as he's about to pull the trigger and watch the life leave my innocent and carefree body?

Maybe kicking up a scene would have been a better idea. Well played Emily, well played.

I can feel his eyes burning into me as I stand frozen, rigidly rooted to the spot. Bloody hell, all I wanted to do was grab a sandwich and a packet of crisps from Marks'. What a way to go, though, death by hunger at the hands of a complete and utter stranger.

"I don't know what you want from me." I whimper, not sure why he hasn't fired and got all of this over and done with yet. "Take it," I say as I hold out my bag, still refusing to meet his eyes.

"Your bag?"

"I know it's not much, a couple of loyalty cards, one seriously maxed out credit card so you'll have no joy with that I'm afraid, but there's a shattered iPhone 7 in there. I'm pretty sure you'd still get a good price for spares and repairs, though."

"Emily, I don't want your bag. I don't want to hurt you."

"You don't?" I ask suspiciously and I finally let out a long gust of air that I didn't realise I was holding in. After a couple more seconds have passed, I finally lift my head up and look at him, not realising that this could all still be some messed up little ploy just so he can get ready to attack.

"No. No, I don't." Scott-Scott shakes his head sincerely and for some strange reason, I think I actually believe him.

Jesus Christ. I really need to have a good old, strong talking to myself. This is ridiculous. My decisions recently haven't been the best, have they? "Well, that's absolutely fan-flipping-tastic. I won't lie, you kind of had me worried for a minute there." I laugh nervously and secretly hope that he doesn't pick up on it. There's nothing these kinds of people like more than weak prey and I refuse to become someone's prey.

"Sorry, it must have been the shock from bumping into you, I guess. I just wanted to know why you've been ignoring me? You just kind of went AWOL all of a sudden, without so much as a warning. I really hope I didn't do anything to offend you? I thought we were getting on great and then…"

Wow. This guy must be on some serious crack. He clearly wasn't joking when he said he thought he knew me? Even though I've told him that I haven't got a clue who he is, he's still fairly insistent. If he's not a hit-man, then who the hell is he? "Look, I've got absolutely no idea who you are. I really wish I did so that I could help put you out of your misery, but I have never, ever spoken to you in my whole entire life. That I am one hundred percent sure of."

"Not in person, no." He continues and he's really getting more creepier and creepier by the second. I flinch back a little as he rams his phone right in front of my face, which personally I find highly rude. How hard is it for people to use their manners these days?

So, that's what he was grabbing out of his pocket. "See, that's you is it not?" He demands, shoving it a little bit closer, causing me to step backwards, unsure of what I'm going to bang into.

I try my best to adjust my eyes, a little hazy from the close proximity and… wow. He's not bloody lying. It's me. There I am staring back at the real me from his phone. How has this guy got my picture on his phone, and more importantly, why?

"Yes…" I nod in disbelief as his phone continues to creep closer and closer to my eyes and he even gives it a little shake for added effect as if to say, *'see, I told you so.'* "But one question. Why do you have *my* picture on *your* phone?"

He shrugs and looks at me as if I have just asked the most bizarre and most random question ever known to man. "Because *you* sent it to me." He replies, but he looks just as confused as I feel.

Well, this is turning out to be pretty eventful, isn't it? "Say what now?"

The temperature drops just as a big gust of wind sweeps around us. Bloody perfect. I wanted to be back home and settled by the time the snow hits. Mr. Jones may have warned me about it a few days before, but he wasn't lying when he said that there was going to be a mass downpour of the wicked white stuff.

"Faithful flats, today might just be the day that I lose you," I say to myself silently and my chest aches at the thought of such a horrific loss. We've been through so much and it'd be a real shame for us to separate. These shoes have been there for me when no one else has, protecting me no matter what the situation.

"Emily if you're not interested anymore just tell me. It's okay I get it, shit happens. The last thing I want to do is stand here looking like an absolute knob for no reason."

I turn my attention back to Scott-Scott, completely freaked out by this whole situation. Maybe if the two of us had met under different circumstances, I'd probably find him pretty cute. But now? Most definitely not. I'm afraid he's now right up there with nipple man. I can't help but shudder at the thought.

"I won't lie to you Scott. You're kind of scaring me here, pal. I don't know you from Adam, yet you seem to know a lot about me."

"Right." He says as his hand swoops over his jaw. The poor bloke looks utterly defeated. "Okay, well I guess there's not much left for me to say is there?"

"Not really." I half smile, trying my best to sound as sympathetic as one can in this kind of messed up situation. In all honestly, though, I'm not even convincing myself. Deciding enough is enough, desperate to get out of the icy cold, I place my right foot forward as I say, "I wish I could say that it's been nice meeting you, but it's really been a little bit weird, hasn't it? Oh, and please could you delete that photo of me as well? I don't know who sent it to you, but I can assure you that whoever it was wasn't me."

"Do you think that someone's pretending to be you?" He gasps.

Strangely enough, that thought hadn't even entered my mind, well not until now. I suppose alarm bells should have been firing off from every direction as soon as he rammed my picture in my face. But, what with a crazed loon taking over my personal space and the cold winter air threatening to crack my poor, neglected nipples, it just wasn't really on top of my agenda.

"I guess it looks that way," I say sombrely. Who the hell would want to pretend to be me anyway? Yes, I'm not too modest to admit that I can be pretty freaking awesome at the best of times, but trust me, no one would want to be me 24/7. Bloody hell, even I'd love to have a break from being me from time to time, but I just can't seem to catch that break. No matter what I do, it just doesn't seem to be happening for me. "Actually, before I go, could you tell me how we've *apparently* been communicating?"

"Huh?"

"Well…" I say slowly, "you've already said that we've never spoken face to face before, so how is it that we were talking?"

"POF." He replies, very matter of fact.

"Excuse me?" I snap, slightly offended by his response. "Are you trying to be funny? You have images of me on your phone, images that do not belong to you and only god knows what else and you don't even have the balls to tell me how or where you acquired them?" Numerous passers-by slower their pace so they can have a right good old eavesdrop at my squealing voice. Why the hell am I still even stood here trying to argue the toss with a total stranger? It's clearly getting me nowhere and I should have just carried on walking as soon as he started talking to me.

"POF. Don't tell me that you don't know what it is?" No, I bloody well don't. Why else would I be asking? "Plenty. Of. Fish." He continues, not really paying any attention to the confused expression on my face, or maybe I just look constipated, who knows? "You know, plenty more fish in the sea and all that? It's an online dating website. Clearly, it's not you that's been messaging me."

"And the penny finally drops." I say, my voice laced with sarcasm. Finally, this Dude seems to be getting it loud and clear in his deluded little mind that I'm not the person that he thinks I am.

"Look, I'm sorry. I'll delete everything, even though I'll be gutted to see those awesome tit-pics go." He smirks right at me. The cocky little shit.

He isn't smirking for long when my palm quickly connects with his face. *"Ouch."* Shit, that hurt. "I'm sorry," I say questioningly. Because well, I'm not a violent person, but damn it felt good to let loose for a second. *Fucking pervert*.

"I'm out of here." He mouths while hurriedly walking backwards, yet he never takes his shocked wide eyes away from mine until he's completely out of sight, swallowed up by the mass crowds of one of London's busiest streets.

Chapter 13

Rachel. Bloody Rachel.

I'm going to physically kill her when I get my hands on her. How could she do this? How could she do this to me, of all people?

I couldn't get Scott and the whole dating site thing out of my head on the way home. It all just kept on spinning round and round on repeat, like a vicious cycle and with each passing second my anger grew increasingly, which is rare for me and never a good sign for the person who caused me to feel this way.

Now I know that Rachel's super keen on all this dating malarkey, I've witnessed her in action numerous times, but to actually go out of her way and open some random account in my name and then to have the audacity to pretend to be me, saying and sending only God knows what is taking it to a whole new level. A level that should never be reached when said person is supposed to be your best friend.

Sure, she added me to Tinder and created a monster in the process and yes, she set me up on a blind date, which just so happened to be with the most sexiest man that I have ever had the pleasure of scanning my eyes over, and that was all fine. It was A-Okay; because no matter how much I tried to plead with her eventually I consented, but not to this. Frigging hell, I didn't even know about any of this and that in itself isn't fair.

I mean we're supposed to be friends, yet she's off having a jolly old time sexting away with random strangers and sending over sordid pictures of me. To get a kick out of it at my expense? A little ego boost? She's got a hell of a lot to answer for, that's for sure.

I'm absolutely livid. For all Rachel knew, that Scott guy could have kidnapped me or anything. Would anyone have noticed that I'd gone, completely disappeared? No, because all the evidence is on bloody Rachel's phone and not mine. Me and my poor faithful flats could have been right up shit street and no one would have been none the wiser. I shudder just thinking out it.

I arrive at my garden gate just as big, thick, white flakes begin to fall down around me. Wow, talk about timing. That's possibly the only positive thing that's happened to me today. I really can't wait to get inside, throw on my favourite penguin pyjama's and shut the whole world out for a little while. Surely, I'm owed at least that much? Well, maybe I could throw in a couple of bars of chocolate, some Haagen-Dazs ice-cream, and a little bit of shitty tele and then the balance would be evened out ever slightly. But only just.

I spot Mr Jones peeping out from behind his blinds and I give him a little wave as my feet crunch against the gravel. It certainly looks like he's got the right idea. At least he's safe and warm, inside nice and cosy. I'd hate to think of him being poorly, especially this time of year. I'd hate for anyone to get ill, but I'm quite fond of Mr Jones. No matter how loud he blasts his music, he's always there, looking out for me. It wouldn't surprise me if my Grandma has him vetted before she bought the place.

The minute my foot is through the front door I grab my post and the quickly turn the lock, making my disconnection with the outside complete.

… And breathe.

There's nothing better than coming home to a warm and peaceful house. Especially when the voices inside your head are constantly screaming and getting way out of control. I don't know who they are or where they've come from, but they really need to pipe down, and fast.

Pulling out my now battered once was not so long ago shiny brand new iPhone 7, I notice a message from Rachel which I completely forgot about earlier, just before I all too physically bumped into Scott-Scott. I tell you what though, it's a bloody good job my screen's broken because right now I really don't want to know what she's got to say. It'll all be fake bullshit anyway.

Some things I'd risk slicing my fingers open for, but right now Rachel isn't one of them. Now that's something that I never imagined I would ever say. Today is just bursting at the seams with surprises. Plus, the little witch still owes me a new bloody phone, too. If it wasn't for her and her stupid online dating addiction then I wouldn't have been on Tinder to start with and my phone wouldn't have jumped right out of my hands onto the table, would it? Speaking of which, I'm not doing all that bad with my Tinder addiction, it's been what, two days since my last swipe? My thumbs could do with a little work out, though. But overall, I'm actually surprising myself.

"No Emily, because that would then make you a hypocrite as you would fall right into Rachel's category."

"I don't want to think about Rachel right now."

For God sake, I bloody wish that alter ego of mine would piss off. She doesn't pipe up when it comes to stopping me from making stupid decisions. No, she sits back and silently watches from the side- lines only to goad me about it at the most inconvenient times. I really don't like her all that much anymore.

As I rifle through my bag, searching high and low for my favourite chap stick I stumble across Noah's mystery package. Oh, Noah, sexy, hot as hell Noah. He is so swoon worthy, it's unreal. I wonder what it could be and why in the name of man he would be sending me of all people a package. I hold it ever so delicately, not too sure if it's worthy of my clumsy hands. And to think that Scott-Scott could have had off with it and I would have never known what was inside.

Uh, the suspense is killing me. I've not been so excited about a surprise since Santa brought me my first ever Polly pocket. I don't care what anyone says, Polly pockets were the shit, even more so when they brought out the magnetic ones. All of a sudden, my Polly Pocket was real, actually alive and she was all mine. I'm pretty sure my Mum's still got a few of mine stored away in the loft. Bloody hell, those were the days when the only thing you needed to worry about was whether you'd be allowed to play with it after tea, or not. What I'd do to be able to go back in time. I'd make sure that I cherished those carefree moments, because growing up isn't all that it's cracked up to be.

Unable to contain my giddy little self anymore, I gently tear off the expensive looking wrapping paper and gasp loudly as my brain takes in its contents. Jesus, just when I thought my very own Thor couldn't get any more perfect, he goes and throws something like this into the mix.

For crying out loud, I don't even know the guy, yet this is possibly the most nicest, most thoughtful gift I have ever received. *"Thor..."* I swoon again and a humongous grin spreads across my face. I'm like a fat kid in a sweet shop as my hands tenderly caress the cold, grey metal. Oh, it's so beautiful; so new and not a single smashed screen in sight.

I pause a minute, reluctantly pulling my eyes away from this new and very much wanted addition to my life and wonder if I can really accept this gift. I mean, never in my life has anyone bought me something as great as this. The only thing that Tyler ever bought for me was reduced to almost free wilted flowers and that was only so he didn't end up getting a headache about never treating me to anything. Looking back, I don't think I can ever remember a time when he took me out for a meal and actually paid for it. But alas, I was blind and in love, so I would always forgive him anything. Well, within reason, which he soon came to realise in time.

Now this, this shiny little 4.7 inches of goodness is too much to accept from someone that I have only just met. Oh God, it's breaking my heart at just the thought of having to give it back.

"I'd love you for all eternity and I know that I could give you a good home." I murmur, suddenly sounding like Smeagol when it comes to his precious. *"I'd be more careful and take good care of you and not be so reckless this time."* And just like that, my decision is made. My shiny, super brand spanking new iPhone 7 is staying and it's all mine.

How on earth will I ever be able to say thank you to him? I guess all I can do is hope that he pops into Rachel's again. If not, I'll have to go for the big guns and see if she has his number. Now that's a first, little old me asking for someone's number. She'll probably think I've got it majorly bad. Oh, well. Maybe that's something that I'm just going to have to chance.

"Bollocks. I guess I could do that if I was speaking to her" I remind myself. Ugh, why does everything have to be so bloody complicated? On a plus note, I guess this must mean that he's pretty keen on a second date? I don't think I did anything too embarrassing the other night, either, so here's hoping.

Something catches my eye as I go to grab the luxurious wrapping paper from the kitchen worktop. Is that what I think it is? Sure enough, a small rectangular card slides out. I go to pick it up and then stop. Do I really want to see what's written on there? Maybe the gift wasn't really for me and Rachel just assumed? Its stupid I know, but a teeny tiny part of me is scared to read it. I mean what can you possibly say to someone to explain all of this? He clearly doesn't know that he's reached way over maximum brownie points after replacing the one and only love of my life.

"Jesus Christ Emily, grow some bloody balls and have a look. It won't bite you." I scold myself. Oh well, here goes. I close my eyes tightly as I turn the thick card over in my hands before opening them again and trying to

work out his not so eloquent scrawl. Well, I guess you can't have everything, can you? If he did, I'd definitely be getting worried.

'Emily, I'm sorry I startled you and in turn caused you to break your phone. Please accept this gift as my way of an apology. Noah.

P.S. My number is already saved in your contacts if you ever feel like giving me a call?'

Wow. Just wow. I have no words. Absolutely none.

I read and re-read his little note over and over again, thinking that eventually it will disappear and I imagined all of this. This stuff just doesn't happen to me, like ever. If I wasn't super mad at Rachel right now, then she'd be the first person I'd be calling to give all the juicy gossip too. But I am mad; I'm super mad and I don't want to say anything to her in the heat of the moment that I might just live to regret or can't take back. No, I think I'm best to sleep on things before I speak to her. We're definitely going to need a calm and relaxed environment when I start grilling her.

~*~

I press my home screen to see that my brand new, shiny, toy is fully charged and ready to go and to make things that little bit better and easy for me, what with iCloud being so flipping awesome and because I'm a lazy and forgetful cow, everything that I need has automatically transferred over. Everything plus one additional item…

… Noah's number.

My thumb idly hovers over his name, but I can't find the courage to hit the call button. Plus, it's gone 9 pm and now might not be a sociable time for him to chat. He could be doing anything. Probably something much more exciting than waiting for little old me to call. What would I even say to him anyway? Knowing my luck his note was more than likely added as a polite touch.

"But why would he leave his number in your contacts, stupid?" My inner bitch comes back to life at just the right time. I guess she does have a point. Maybe it's because he genuinely felt bad for me because my phone went to shit right before his very eyes.

I guess I could always send a text. There's no pressure that way. I've been polite in responding and thanking him for my new phone and then the ball's left in his court if he wants to pursue things any further.

I blow out a deep, frustrated breath. It's like being back in bloody high school all over again when I didn't know if James Johnson really liked me or not, or if it was all just some silly bet that he had with his mates. I give my head a big wobble and begin to type. You're almost thirty for crying out loud Emily. It's about time you started to act like a fully grown adult at times.

'Hey, Noah. It's me, Emily.' Crap, is that too formal? Who cares, it's just a text. Get a grip. *'Thank you very much for the phone. It's beyond generous and you really shouldn't have. I really appreciate the kind gesture, though.'* I read it over and over again, before finally adding *'I really enjoyed the other night, hopefully, we can do it again sometime soon?'*

I hit send before I can back out of it and I try my best not to focus on my blank screen. It's only been a minute and I'm pretty sure that he's got more important things to do with his time than to sit around waiting for me to contact him. To my surprise, almost instantly my phone beeps to life in my hands and when I look down there it is, a message from Noah.

'I'm glad you like it and you're most welcome. Tomorrow, 8 pm. Be free.'

Well, that's a bit up front, isn't it? Be free? Not are you free, but be free. Does he think I don't have anything better to do with my time? Not that he'd be wrong, but still. Does my body language scream out 'loner' to the people around me?

Yes, there's no denying that Noah is hot as hell and yes, there's also no denying that I really enjoyed spending time with him the other night, but I really don't like it when guys become full of themselves. It makes them become obnoxious and arrogant pricks and I really don't like wasting my time on them. Bloody be free. The absolute cheek of some people. He's starting to sound like Matt.

"But he looks just like Chris Hemsworth so he can be as arrogant as he likes." Oh, there she is again, piping right up when I really don't need or want her to.

Yes, yes, he does and I know that I'm screwed either way, but one thing I don't want is to come across as easy because that's one thing that I'm not and have never been.

"You were with Matt, so what's the difference, Mother Teresa?"

Ignoring my nasty, unwanted inner bitch I type out a quick reply. *'Tomorrow? Let me check and get back to you. Emily. X'*

I don't want any man to think that they can just click their fingers and I'll happily just come running like a flaming poodle. That will never happen, ever. I'm my own person and I fully intend on staying that way.

Without a doubt, today has definitely been one hell of a crazy arse day. What I need now is a good fumble with Vinnie, leading up to a delectable stress relieving orgasm and a good night's sleep. Everything feels so much better after those two, somehow.

Chapter 14

Knock… knock… knock…

"Go away." I shout out while dragging my quilt over my head to block out the noise. Who in their right bloody mind starts hammering on people's doors at this ungodly hour? All I wanted was a little lie in, but oh no, it looks like that's not about to happen.

Knock… knock… knock…

The tapping continues and it sounds like it's beginning to get louder and louder. Annoyingly, whoever's out there isn't about to let up anytime soon. Unwillingly admitting defeat, I throw my covers back begrudgingly and drag myself up and out from beneath my cosy hideaway.

Last night's binging session is laid out all around me, reminding me just how much of a fat, depressed, lonely old pig I really am. Half a bag of family size Doritos stare back at me along with numerous empty Galaxy wrappers and a share size Malteaser box. Seriously, I have no shame at all. Not one little bit.

Do I feel guilty? Hell no, not a chance. After yesterday I believe I earned every goddamn calorie and then some. The way I see it, it was a little treat and we all have to indulge every once in a while, otherwise, what's the point to life?

I swing the door open just before my unwanted visitor is able to hammer on it again, catching her with her right arm slightly raised, ready to go for gold.

"Fucking hell, you look like shit."

"You've seen better days too." I snap back as the slimline creature snakes around me and enters my home.

Why, oh why did I have to answer? I should have just stuck my headphones in and pressed shuffle on Spotify.

"Now that's not very nice, is it?" Smiling gleefully, Rachel continues to delve further into my house and the sucker that I am, reluctantly follow suit. "What happened to you calling me yesterday, you promised?"

Unable to bite my tongue much longer, my inner bitch rears her ugly head and explodes out of my body. "What happened? I'll tell you what happened Rachel. Fucking Scott happened." I watch her carefully, waiting for the guilt to creep across her perfectly contoured face but it doesn't happen. Instead, she just looks at me like a gormless person, albeit a beautiful gormless person, but still, gormless all the same. "You know, Scott-Scott." I add, hoping this will make something click in her head.

"Who? Oh... is this some new guy that we need to discuss? I've got to admit Emily, considering you were totally against this online dating malarkey, you ain't half working through them. Girl, you're on fire. I'm super proud of you."

"Rach, I'm really not in the mood to play games. Of course, you know who I'm talking about."

"Nope, honestly doll, I haven't got a clue. But, as soon as I've made these latte's you can bet your pert little bottom that you'll be telling me all about him."

"I'll take the latte, but not your bullshit." I mutter, just loud enough for her to hear me.

"Excuse me?" Rachel squeals and spins right around to face me. "What did you just say? Why are you being so nasty to me? What have I done?"

"I don't know. Maybe you'd like to tell me why you would go behind my back?" I stare her down, waiting for her to crack ever so slightly but she's still looking at me like I've lost the plot and I'm blowing my shit for no apparent reason. This is typical Rachel behaviour. God knows that I love her dearly, but at times she doesn't half do things without thinking them through properly.

"Go behind your back? What the hell are you talking about? You were fine when you left yesterday. What's gotten into you?"

I take a seat at the kitchen table and drop my head into my hands. Everything is just getting too much for me. Why does my life always seem to fall apart, I mean look at me, I'm single, almost thirty and I've as good as lost my job. Not only that, but my best friend clearly feels that sorry for me, she had to set up an online dating account to get me a man. Talk about a major confidence boost. "Rachel, do you really need to lie to me? Did you ever think that I wouldn't find out?" Of course she did. That's why she's gone out of her way to do it.

"Take this. Now I'm going to tell you this once and once only so make sure you listen carefully. I haven't got a flaming clue what you're going on about so you need to quit the bitch act and tell me what the hell's going on here, otherwise I'm going to turn around and walk right out of that door." She says and slams my latte down in front of me. "And I won't be coming back until you sort yourself out." I look up to see that she's staring me down.

I match her bitch face with my own and say, "POF. Plenty of fish... does that ring any bells?"

"Oh God, you haven't gone on there have you? I thought you were only just getting to grips with Tinder." Rachel sits down next to me and her expression softens. "You don't need to get greedy you know." Her hand gently rests on my shoulder and she gives it a little squeeze. "Oh Emily, what am I going to do with you?"

"Rach, come on. Please don't play games. What you've done isn't fair and it's completely uncalled for."

"What do you mean, what I've done. Just because I helped you get to grips with Tinder doesn't mean you can blame everything else on me too."

"I know you created my profile." I say flatly and it breaks my heart to see her next to me, still lying to my face. Maybe she was doing it out of the kindness of her heart, trying to give me a little shove, but the fact that she's still lying to me hurts more than anything else. I thought we were better than that.

"I haven't created anything. You need to start from the beginning, Emily. I don't know what's running around in your little head, but I really don't like where this is going." She snaps and her pretty little face becomes all prissy.

Well here goes. Hopefully, I can keep my calm because I really need to get this off my chest. If not, the anger is just going to keep building and building until I explode and there's nothing left of me apart from an empty shell in a nut ward. "Yesterday when I was on my way back from the Doctors I went barrelling into some guy. Usually, I would have muttered a quick apology and been on my way, but… well, I just couldn't."

"Why not?" She says encouragingly.

"I couldn't because he said he knew me. He knew my name and everything, but I didn't know him. I'd never seen his face before in my life. I really thought he was going to kidnap me or turn out to be some kind of hit man or something. It was horrendous."

"Emily people mistake other people all the time. It's no big deal. I don't see what you're getting all worked up for."

"It's no big deal? Rachel, are you even listening to me? He knew my name and to make matters worse, he shoved his bloody phone in my face and there I was, staring back at myself." I pause briefly, just to take a sip of my drink before continuing. "The guy had pictures of me on his phone, which by the way I'd apparently sent to him amongst other things over this dating thingy majig."

"But you didn't?" Rachel asks and she looks just as confused as I feel. I'll tell you one thing, she's got an absolute corker of a poker face.

"No, I didn't. But I think I know who did…" I probe again and I wait for her response. "Don't I?"

"Who… wait. Are you saying what I think you're saying? You think that I've been sending things of you to some random guys? Fucking hell Emily, what do you take me for?"

Oh, she looks majorly pissed right now and a small part of me wishes that I didn't say anything. Maybe Rachel didn't set anything up. Maybe I've got it all wrong and I've gone out all guns blazing without asking questions first. "It has to be you."

"Why, because I'm an evil vindictive bitch like that? Emily, you're my best friend. Why the hell would I go behind your back like that? Do you even know me at all?"

"I don't know, do I? Why do you think I'm so angry?"

"You're angry? You've got no idea how I feel, let me tell you." Rachel shouts back at me without even pausing for air.

"But you're the only one who knows all of my details and I know you're obsessed with all that online dating stuff. You were so excited when you set that other one up."

"Yes, I enjoy it. Yes I have lots of fun on it and yes, it kills time when I'm bored shitless, but to do that to you without you knowing? That's not my style at all. Have you even had a look at the profile to see what's on there? Is it my writing style?"

No I haven't. Maybe that's the first thing that I should have done. At least that way I may have been able to decipher if it was Rachel's writing style like she said. God, now I feel like such a muppet. I shake my head at Rachel, unable to talk and even though a small pitiful smile breaks free on her lips, I can still tell that she's super mad at me. To be fair, I'd be pretty mad at me too.

Chapter 15

"Do you really think that I'd write something like that?" Rachel asks, trying to control her breathing between fits of laughter. There's no stopping her. She's physically howling like a bloody banshee. "Oh, honestly Emily; this is absolute gold. I didn't do it but I'll tell you what, I'd bloody love to shake hands with whoever did."

"I'm glad you're highly amused." I reply. What a cow. She's still laughing and I give her a hard-ish jab to the side. Bitch. She's supposed to be on team Emily, not team Emily wannabe.

After I'd refused point blank to look myself up on this 'Plenty of fish' thingy-majig, Rachel went straight in, all guns blazing and fired my Mac Book right up and off she went on her merry bloody way. It took everything I had to finally sit down and take a peek. Jesus, it's absolutely mortifying, to say the least. Ultimate cringe and it's making me want to vomit.

Where do I start? First off, I don't know where my profile picture came from or who took it, but I really couldn't look more slutty if I'd tried. It must have been photoshopped or something because never, in the history of man have I ever worn a red lip. I might be pale, but that colour just makes me look ill. Plus. my lips look like they've had one too many rounds of a collagen injection. However, on a more positive note, my tit's look pretty impressive and my eyebrows are on point.

Now, if I was a man and I had a fully functioning penis; out of ten I'd definitely give myself one.

It's not the picture though that's got Rachel howling. Oh no, she fully approves of that. No, it's my bio that's the highlight of the day.

The crap that's written on there is so unbelievable that I have to keep reading it over and over again, to try and allow it all to sink into my frazzled brain. It reads:

'Hi, I'm Emily, my friends call me Em but I'm more than happy to be anything that you want me to be. I like my men just like my wine; mighty fine and thoroughly matured.

My hobbies include practicing the Karma Sutra as often as physically possible. It's so much more entertaining than your average yoga session and much more beneficial to your mental and overall health.

I'm a very active person, in every way possible and I'll happily keep you entertained for as long as you can handle...'

It doesn't end there, though. It just goes on and on and on. I bet I've had some right nut jobs trying to hook up with me on here.

"Hey Emily, there's a mobile number on here you know and it's not yours." Rachel gasps and excitedly points to the screen. "I think I'll give it a call and see what happens."

"But it's not me, you nutter."

"No shit Sherlock. But, think outside the box for a minute bright spark. Whoever is behind all of this is obviously contacting them through this number." Her eyes grow wide as she waits for the light to come on and it click. Finally, it does.

"Oh…" I say when my poor frazzled brain eventually registers what she's saying. "Bloody Karma Sutra, though. I'm lucky if I get any missionary action."

"Well according to this little beauty, you're quite the sex guru. You little naughty minx, you."

"Oh piss off and get off your high horse. Is it wine o'clock yet?" I ask loudly and she shrugs casually at me.

"I guess it's five o'clock somewhere."

I'm dressed and I'm almost ready to face the big bad world outside. Not that I've really got much choice with Rachel by my side, egging me on every step of the way.

I feel dreadful, I really do. I feel like such a nasty cow for automatically assuming the worst and straight off going mad at her like that. To be fair, though, in my defense I've had quite a lot to deal with over the past couple of weeks. Actually, scrap that, the past twelve months have seen better days. But onwards and upwards as they say. That's the motto that I'm going with right now. Surely one of these days it's got to get better, or a little bit easier.

I find Rachel exactly where I left her about forty-five minutes ago. She's not moved an inch. Her small delicate frame is still hunched over my Mac Book and she looks thoroughly engrossed with whatever it is that she's reading.

"Hey, you." I smile and take a seat next to her at the kitchen table where she's currently set up shop. I'm not surprised when she doesn't look at me, just grunts a little in acknowledgment. I guess that's something at least. "Look, I'm really sorry about earlier. I shouldn't have jumped the gun like that." I'm genuinely sorry and I'll admit that I feel really small and vulnerable right now. I also feel horrific for treating my best friend the way that I did, and all without so much as a second thought. "Still friends?" I whisper.

"Always." She turns her head slightly to look at me and she gently places her left hand over mine. " Yes, I won't lie, you've been a complete and utter bell-end about all of this, but luckily for you, I know what you're like. Next time just ask me, okay?"

"I promise." I smile back and just like that, I feel instantly lighter. Like some of my sins have been repented. But only some.

"Good. Now that's all cleared up and you finally look half human, it's time for us to get going."

"Erm, go where?" With Rachel around, I knew that she'd have something on the agenda, but the glint in her eye right now as I look at her scares the living crap out of me. She knows that I hate surprises. Maybe this is payback? Yep, definitely payback. I wouldn't put anything past her.

"That's why I came over. Well, at least it was right up until you went all bat-shit bipolar Brian on me."

"I wasn't that bad." I exclaim, trying to defend myself and claim my innocence.

"Oh, you were. Believe me. Anyway, that's done with now so let's just forget about it. It's in the past." She flutters her eyelashes at me because she knows she has me hook, line, and sinker right now. "Look, I know that you've had it pretty tough recently and I have watched you try to hide it as best you can, but lady, you can't kid a kidder. I just think that you could do with a break from all the drama, so... I booked us a little surprise."

And there it is. That dreaded word; *surprise*. "Can we not just stay here and hide?" I ask, hoping that she doesn't take offence to my idea. After all, she seems to have gone to some trouble to make this little break special for me.

"Had you asked me that when I walked in, I would have dragged you out of the house kicking and screaming, but I have to tell you after looking at some of these profiles on here, I kind of want to stay and find out more, myself."

Wow. I didn't expect her to come out with something like that, that's for sure. "Really, can we?" I ask, full of excitement at the pure possibility of being a hermit for the day, if not everyday.

"Erm... no." She says flatly.

Ugh, I hate it when she gets all arsey on me. It doesn't suit her one bit and she bloody well knows it too.

"You know, most of these guys probably have wives and kids at home," I mutter bitterly.

"You know you're probably right, but there's a pretty good chance that there are some good eggs hiding amongst that basket too. You've just gotta rifle through all those feathers to find them."

"What happened to Doug?" I ask quizzically.

"He's still around. I've just not got the urge to sit on him as much as I did before, that's all. This chick could do with some fresh meat."

"Maybe you just need to go out and try having a conversation with him. You know attraction isn't always just about the sex." I add in and surprise myself at the words coming from my mouth. Where have I gone?

"I know, I know. I'm just not sure that he's right for me, that's all."

"Rachel, you won't know unless you give it a try, will you?"

Rachel's head whips around to face me fully and for a second she looks exactly like the girl from the exorcist. A face that I never want to see again for as long as I live. I couldn't sleep for months after watching that horrific thing. "Well look at you." She squeaks and I slowly pull my body back into the chair, not knowing which move she's going to make next. "You've changed your tune, haven't you?"

"God no" I might sound like I have, but I certainly haven't. "Don't get go getting your wires crossed, men are still dickheads at the best of times and that's one thing that I'll always stand by. But you, you're a weirdo and you love men no matter what. So, what's really happening with the two of you, then?"

"Speaking of men, when are you going to fill me in on the hot hunk of a man that goes by the name of Noah?" Oh, nice. I know what she's doing. There's nothing like a good old change of subject and I suppose it's in my best interest to humour her since I'm still treading on thin ground. But do I really want to? Now that's the question…

"I don't really know." I tell her honestly. Truthfully, I don't think she's really paying that much attention to me as she's still completely zoned out on the computer. I could tell her that we ran off and got married and enjoyed an amazing orgy and she probably wouldn't even bat an eyelid. Instead, I say, "There's not much to tell."

"You sure about that? Surely you wouldn't lie to your best friend, would you? What about that gift he gave to me for you yesterday?" There's no way that you can try and get anything passed this one.

Crap. I'd actually forgotten all about his little gift until Rachel just brought it up. How the hell could I forget something like that? "Oh, that? Well, it's not your average present, that's for sure."

Now I've got her attention. Her full, undivided attention. Her pretty little face is waiting for me to expose all and she's not sitting patiently. She taps her fingers as she waits for me to spill everything. "Come on then, don't be a carrot dangler. Hey, it wasn't something kinky like a personalised butt plug, was it? You know thinking about it, he does kind of give off that whole alpha domineering type."

"Rachel, don't be so crude." I shout. "Your mind is absolute filth. Maybe you should calm yourself and take it out of the gutter."

"Chocolates? He doesn't strike me as the boring and predictable type Emily. Please don't shatter my expectations whatever you do."

I can't help but laugh at her. Everything, no matter how big or small always seems to be dramatized with her. "No." I manage to say in between laughter, "not chocolates. I guess you could say it's more of an item that has a much more personal use. Something that I absolutely love more than anything else in the world."

"Coffee? What, did he get you, some super awesome beans? Maybe that's why he's single, because he's crap at buying gifts."

"Not quite... more like an iPhone 7." I squeal and clap my hands with joy. Oh it's so beautiful and precious and I promise to cherish and look after it every single day.

"Shut the front door. Why would he buy you an iPhone? You've already got a new one."

"Did... I did have one." Even though it's now been replaced, a dull ache still burns deep in my chest when I think about its short little life. "I did have one until he walked over to me, oozing sex appeal on our date and I flustered like the clumsy cow that I am and like a right bloody tit I let go of it and it went flying out of my hands and shattered on the table right before my eyes. Honestly Rach, there was nothing that I could have done to prevent it. My heart was in my mouth and I thought I was about to die too. It's not something that I ever want to experience ever again in my entire life."

"You bloody clumsy cow. I told you to get a decent case."

"Rachel, eggs these days are free range because it's not natural for the hens to be caged up all the time. It's exactly the same principle for phones you know. They weren't designed to be stuck in a cold and unsightly case. Ever."

"Yeah, something's really not right with you." I hate it when she looks at me with those eyes. When she looks at me like that I sometimes have to stop and question my sanity, but I know that I'm not crazy. She just doesn't understand my personal view on the world sometimes, that's all. Like everyone, I guess we have to agree to disagree from time to time.

"Anyway, he probably just felt guilty and he's clearly got more money than sense."

"Or maybe, just maybe, he could be a decent guy and wanted to make sure that he could get in touch with you again."

"Hmmm, maybe you're right. When I opened it up his number was already saved in the contacts list."

"And have you called him? At least sent him a thank you message?" Rachel practically hyperventilates in my face. Dear God woman, give me a bloody break. Anyone would think it was her going on dates with him.

"Calm down, Jesus. And yes, I did. I texted him last night if you must know."

"Oh…" A mischievous grin spreads across her lips and her whole face lights up. "What did he say? Emily, he's so sexy and swoon-worthy." Her eyes wander off as she imagines only God knows what.

"He'd like to take me out again tonight." I say, and something that I've not experienced for a long time runs through my body.

Nerves… actual nerves.

Chapter 16

We've been driving for what feels like an absolute age and there's no way that Rachel's going to let up anytime soon. I've asked her numerous times to tell me where we're going and I've even gone as far as using reverse psychology too and nothing is working. It's driving me completely insane.

There has to be something that will make her crack. I just don't know what it is.

"It's a surprise," is all that she keeps telling me. Bloody hell, we've been best friends for almost twenty years and she knows how much I hate surprises. "All will be revealed soon enough."

The suspense is killing me, literally. God only knows where we could end up. This isn't the first time that she's decided to take me on a surprise road trip. Let's just say what should have been a two night glamping trip ended up being a five night stay in the local hospital. Somehow I don't think either one of us would like to repeat that experience ever again.

"Glamping?" I remind her and I watch her whole body shudder at the memory and an evil smile takes over my face.

"Never again, at least not on my watch. If *you* want to do that again, then by all means feel free, but don't think for a second that I'll be joining in." I'm sure her complexion has faded a little too.

"Ha. No you're alright. I think I'll live a happy and rather fulfilling life without seconds, thanks." I guess that makes two of us then.

"Hey, I've been wondering. Have you heard from Matt?"

Okay, well that's a drastic change of subject if ever there was one. "No." I reply as calmly as possible, but my voice betrays me by letting of a little high-pitched squeak. "Why do you ask?"

"I just thought he would have been round to see you, you know after..." she wanders off, deciding not to finish her sentence as if she's just said something that she shouldn't have.

Shit. That stupid bloody blabber mouth. So, he's got enough balls to tell everyone and by everyone I'll take a wild stab in the dark and guess he told Mel what went down with us, yet he can't face seeing me? You know, he must find me so repulsive. My hands automatically fall down into my lap and I'm unsure what I'm supposed to say next. I feel used. It's not something that I'm used to feeling, and it's not a nice feeling at all. Honestly, I wouldn't wish it on anyone. Not even Cruella, well, maybe her but she's the devil.

Yes, I was stupid. I allowed him in when I was vulnerable and I dropped my guard around him; something that I haven't done in a long time and I stupidly allowed my heart to rule my head. Now look where that's gotten me. I think it's pretty fair to say that I've lost a friend

I think if I'm being totally honest with myself, which I'm trying to be these days, not that it's really doing me any favours but what can you do? If I'm honest I'm actually a little bit more upset that I'd ever like to acknowledge out loud.

"I thought you two were pretty close, but this? This really shocks me, Emily." Rachel continues waffling while never taking her eyes off the road ahead. Thank god for small mercies. What am I even supposed to say to her? I've only just landed back in her good books after the way that I treated her earlier and any minute now she's going to blow her shit, and maybe a tyre, all because I didn't have the balls to confide in her.

This is the calm before the storm. I can feel it.

"Not as shocked as me, let me tell you." I murmur. "Rach, I knew it was wrong. I knew that I shouldn't have been so stupid and so careless. Believe me, I never intended for any of it to happen. It's just, well, you know how it goes. I was drunk and upset and then one thing just led to another and... oh God, I feel so cheap and used. Now all I'll ever be is just another notch on his bloody never ending bedpost." I stop talking suddenly and finally pull my eyes away from my hands and look at her, waiting for Rachel's reaction.

I needn't have bothered. She doesn't say anything. Bloody hell, she's not even looking at me. I look around and see that we've come to a stop but I don't have time to take in the sights right now, I need to know what's going through her head. I need her to tell me what she's thinking. Surely I've not disgusted her that much.

All too soon, Rachel slowly turns to face me, her hazel eyes burning into mine and her mouth sags open a little. "Wow…" she mouths and right at this moment I don't know if that's a good reaction or bad.

"Exactly." I reply weakly.

"You slept with Matt?" She asks, and she looks really confused. This is not the reaction that I was expecting. Oh God, what have I done? I thought she knew. "Bloody hell Emily, you dark horse. I meant that it was strange that he hadn't been around to see you since all that stuff at work kicked off. You and Matt though. Wow, the two of you actually had sex."

"Oh." It's all I can manage. Well, I've definitely dropped myself in the shit now haven't I? One of these days I might just learn to keep my fat trap shut instead of jumping in all guns blazing.

"Clearly he's been to see you at some point though. When did it happen? Why on earth didn't you tell me?"

"Do we really have to do this now? I thought we were going out for a surprise?" I ask, hoping that somewhere in the bottom of her heart she will empathise with me and let it drop, but I know the answer before it leaves her lips.

"Erm yes. I want answers right now. Plus, you hate surprises anyway so you can't use that as a 'get out of jail free' card." Her face is serious and I know that she means business, especially when she kills the ignition, pulls up the handbrake and cuts the sound of Little Mix from the speakers. I bloody loved that song too.

"Come on Rach. I promise I'll tell you, just not now. It's all still to fresh and too raw for me to talk about. Maybe after a glass of wine?" I throw in, hoping alcohol will sway her decision. But I'm asking the wrong person obviously. I'm the one who seems to be easily swayed when alcohol's thrown into the mix.

"It looks like wine got you into this little predicament in the first place… unless?" she questions.

"Unless what? I'm not a raving alcoholic hooker you know."

Rachel raises a quizzical brow at me and then dubiously shakes her head. "unless this isn't the first time that this has happened. You could be late night hook-up's or friends with benefits for all I know. Jesus Emily, has this got anything to do with your suspension? Please be honest with me and tell me now if the two of you have been caught getting down and dirty at work or something."

"God, no. What do you take me for?" I ask, highly offended at her automatic assumption. I'm nothing but professional at all times in the work place. Well, give or take a couple of times when I've had a low down – showdown with Cruella, but that's different. I always have been and I always will be. Yes, it may not seem like it right now, but usually I've got a bloody good set of morals and I always try to use them on a daily basis. "It was just the once, a stupid drunken fumble after one too many glasses of wine. I didn't even know that he was coming over until he knocked on my door totally unannounced that night I'd been suspended and I guess one thing just kind of led to another." My mind wanders back to that night briefly, but Rachel brings me right out my wayward thoughts almost instantly.

"Oh Emily, I knew that something like this would happen eventually. It was only a matter of time. After all, he's always wanted to get in your knickers, yet you've always managed to resist his charms."

"Until now." I add glumly.

"Have you tried calling him?"

"Who Matt? Are you insane? Why would I want to go and do something like that?" I ask, well and truly shocked that she'd even expect me to such a thing. Does she really want me to go down to that level? "Rach, there's no point. The way I see it is that he clearly got what he was after and it's a massive bonus that he doesn't have to worry about facing me any time soon at the office. The whole situation is a complete win-win for him."

"Emily, random question, but have you even stopped and thought for a moment to even look at this whole situation from his point of view?"

I watch my best friend closely, half wondering where the hell she's gone and who's replaced her and I don't say a word. Not a single one. Has she been on crack? Why the hell would I want to stop and look at things from his point of view? Trust me, I'd rather not think about what's going through his head right now. I'd probably be disgusted at every single thing. He is a man after all.

"Can we change the subject now, please? It's really not helping me with my anxiety.

"Okay, but maybe he just doesn't know what to say to you. He could be feeling exactly the same as you are."

"What, embarrassed, ashamed... bloody easy?" I highly doubt that. More like I'm one of his accomplishments that he's finally got his hands on.

"You'll never know unless you step up and make the first move." She gives my thigh a big squeeze in encouragement before continuing, "Come on then my little slutty pants, let the fun begin."

Chapter 17

"You like?"

"Are you kidding me? I know I hate surprises, but this place is absolutely amazing. It's exactly what I need."

"I know. That's why I booked it for us, silly. Plus, you'll be all pampered and feeling super fresh just in time for your super-hot date tonight."

"Hmm…" I purse my lips together tightly, unsure if I should verbally express my feelings. Sure, I'm pretty excited to see Noah again, who the bloody hell wouldn't be. Jesus I am human after all, but I'm also crapping my pants too. Yes, we're going on a second date but what if that's it? What if it all ends there, just like that. Who knows he might see right through me and find me pretty boring this time around. After all, I was just a clumsy mare last time. Or, he might just prove me right and end up turning out to be an absolute tosser. My mind is totally cheering on the latter.

This spa is gorgeous. It really is. I've never been to such a beautiful place before. I won't lie, I can really envision myself running away from my horrific excuse of a life and hibernating here permanently. There's probably enough room to house the majority of London too, but I think kidnapping Rachel and Mel would be more than enough to keep me entertained.

Everything about this luxurious place ticks every single one of my boxes. The most important one being privacy. I'm most definitely a city girl, but right now, just the idea of being hidden away inside the walls of a massive castle like building surrounded by nothing but acres upon acres of land gives me a sudden need that I've never experienced before in my entire life and that's including the build up to the final Twilight book. It's without a shadow of a doubt, the ultimate paradise.

"Well it's too bad that you suck major donkey balls and can't even hold down a job then, isn't it?"

"Oh, piss off, you miserable witch." I argue back to my vicious and ugly alter-ego.

"What? If you don't get your act together soon, the only thing that you'll be living out of is a wet, soggy cardboard box."

Before I have a chance to get all deep and personal with my thoughts, Rachel strolls through the door and comes waltzing right over to me, prosecco in one hand and a plush quilted robe in the other. "Here, get this on," she hands me the robe like a giddy little kipper, "then get some of this stuff down your neck. That'll help soothe all your problems, that will."

I gratefully extend my right hand out and snatch it away from her grasp. She's driving, so I guess it looks like this bad boy's all for me. Hey, I'm not complaining.

For a change, today actually looks like it's set to be a good day.

"Thank you." I whisper as Rachel delicately places her petite bottom on the sofa next to me. She's ridiculous, you know. There's no excuse for it at all really.

Even with her hair tied up in a shaggy, really can't be arsed top-knot, she still manages to look gorgeous and there's not a single drop of make-up in sight. I wonder how we have managed to stay best friends for so long.

Me on the other hand, I bloody look like a right tramp who's hit gold in a local charity shop. Honestly, it's that bad that it's even beginning to become a chore to drag my fat lazy arse to the mirror in the morning. Don't even get me started on my poor split ends. If I were to audition for the part of the Scarecrow in the Wizard of Oz, I'd hands down get the part even without doing anything. No amount of Frizz-ease in the land could control this beast, that's a fact.

Oh, what have I become? A wallowing bloody mess, that's what.

"Don't mention it."

"No, I really mean it. I've been so horrible to you and you've just plodded along and taken it all on the chin when you shouldn't have too. There's really no excuse for it and I really don't know why you continue to put up with me. I really don't."

"Honestly?" She laughs. "Neither do I at times, but I'll tell you one thing, my life would be pretty damn boring without you in it and that's a fact."

"Well if you put it like that, fortunately for you it looks like you've hit the best friend jackpot." I say sarcastically and in true Rachel fashion, she just rolls her eyes at me.

Charming…

As I lie here, all relaxed and having a much needed pedicure, drinking all of the prosecco and putting the world to rights with my best friend, a thought suddenly occurs to me. Yes, as strange as it sounds, sometimes that can happen. I know, I even surprise myself. "You know, as relaxed as I am I can't help but feel like a complete knob-head sat here like this."

"Erm… okay. May I ask why?" I can tell just by Rachel's tone that she's a little confused as to where this is going and our beauticians carry on with the treatments. I bet they hear bloody all sorts in this kind of trade.

"Because this bloody face mask smells amazing and all, but it's so tight it feels like it's suffocating my skin.

You know, I bet this is what a knob feels like when it's trapped inside a condom; poor little fellas."

"Emily Parker, has anyone ever told you that you're not quite right in the head? I really do worry about you at times. You know, it really does scare me to think of all the random crap that comes out of your mouth."

"I guess that would make two of us then, but I'm the lucky soul who has to live with it daily."

Chapter 18

"Oh, so now that you're all freshly waxed are you gonna show that sexy son of a bitch Noah the goods, or what?"

Bloody hell. That's Rachel for you, always saying it like it is. We've only been through the front door for five minutes and she's already homing in on me like I'm her prey. You know some people could mistake this kind of behaviour for bullying, but fortunately for her, I know how she is and honestly, I wouldn't have her any other way.

"I don't think that's a wise move, really, do you?" I throw my bag on the table as the nerves start up again at just the mere mention of Noah's name. Will I ever be able to get a grip on my emotions?

"Why the hell not? You've been without for so long. It's hide time you got that Vajayjay of yours back on the market and back in action."

"It's not a bloody piece of meat to be sold to the highest bidder, Rach. I'm quite selective in that department, don't you know."

The look that she's giving me shows me that she feels differently. "Really?"

"Yes, really. Matt doesn't count. He was a, what shall we call him, a mishap?"

"Yeah whatever. But Noah though. I've told you before. He's definitely a shower, I've seen his outline in detail on numerous occasions, so I can only dream of what it must be like when he's got a boner. Oh, it's making me go all funny inside just thinking about it." She spins on the spot and gleefully pulls her hands up to rest just above her chin. "Please. Do it for me. That way you can tell me if he packs the punch that his tight fitted trousers promise."

"Okay, so let me get this straight." I say slowly as I lower myself on to the couch, pulling my legs up and curling them underneath me as I go. "You want me to shag Noah just so that I can tell you what his knob looks and feels like?"

"Hmm mmm. What? Don't look at me like that. I'm a curious soul and it's a win-win situation."

"How the do you work that out you weirdo?"

"It's pretty obvious you numpty. You get to experience some pretty amazing O's and I get to find out if I'm right or not."

"You're being one hundred percent serious right now aren't you? Bloody hell Rach, you're fucking messed up in the head, you."

"Yep." She smiles wickedly at me and I don't know whether to slap her or hug her.

"I've got a better idea. How about you give Doug a quick call? I'm pretty sure he'll be able to occupy you and take your wild and crazy mind off Noah's man bits for a while."

I've got no idea what's going on with these two right now, but Rachel's suddenly turned into some mental, sex crazed mad woman and the one person who could once upon a time sate that need for her was Doug and he doesn't even seem to be touching the sides with her anymore.

"Yeah, maybe." She replies with little emotion in her voice as she tries to shrug me off.

"Come on Rach, what's happened between the two of you?"

"Nothing all that exciting really. I just think it's for the best if the two of us stop seeing each other, that's all."

Okay, well I definitely wasn't expecting her to just come out with something like that. *"I feel like a change,"* or *"He's just not doing it for me anymore."* sounds much more like Rachel's get out quick excuses, but all this? Something just doesn't add up here and I'm going to make sure that I get to the bottom of it.

"First off lady, you can stop with the act. I want answers and I'm going to get them whether you like it or not. You owe me at least that much." I remind her.

"What do you mean?" She shrieks back at me. "I owe you? How do you work that one out?" I wait until she has joined me on the couch, curling her legs underneath her like me before continuing with my beautiful spiel. "In case you forgot, I just had to go through a very humiliating discussion with you that is Matt, didn't I?"

"Hang on a minute. What you're telling me is that I owe you because you finally disclosed something to me that you should have told me straight from the off?"

"Well yeah. Would you have preferred it if I'd given you a call beforehand to give you a quick heads up, or maybe you would have preferred me to leave the call connected so that you could hear us in action?"

"Don't be a bloody smart arse Emily. It doesn't suit you." She scolds. "You know exactly what I mean. You've broken the first rule of friendship, not me so less of the diva act if you will."

"Are you sure that I broke it first? Because from where I'm sitting it seems pretty clear that you're the one who isn't being one hundred percent honest with me."

Rachel watches me quietly for a minute and I can tell just from the set of her face that she's contemplating whether to tell me all the details or not. "I know you better than you know yourself at times Rach. If you didn't like a guy anymore, for whatever reason then you'd just come straight out with it."

"Okay, okay." Her hands fly up into the air and she waves them around, begging me to stop. "Jesus, enough with the shrink act. That shit's nothing but torture."

"So spill. It'll be less painful that way, I promise." I stare her down and it finally looks like my tactics have worked.

"Ugh. Where do I start? Why did everything have to get so complicated?"

Yes, one to Emily. Keep talking Rachel and we'll finally get to the bloody bottom of this. "Have you honestly not learned a thing from me and my experiences? Shit gets complicated because he's a man and he has a penis. You and I both know that those things are trouble and that's trouble with a capital T."

"It was just supposed to be a bit of fun. You know, a little bit of *'how's your uncle'* whenever we felt like it. Always having someone readily available as a plus one with no hidden strings attached. God Emily, it was like living the dream. Either one of us could happily walk away when things became too much, or we needed a little head space. The best thing was that we always knew where we stood with each other, no matter what."

"So, what changed?" Wow, if I thought I was confused about this whole predicament before, it's got nothing on how I'm feeling right now.

"To put it bluntly, we did. Both of us changed and now it's all messed up and gone to shit and I don't know what to do about it all. I've never been in this kind of situation before."

"Oh…" is all that I can say as she sucks her bottom lip in, desperately trying to prevent the wobble from creeping in. Blimmin' heck, she's really upset about all this.

The thing with Rachel is that even though she can be quite guarded, her eyes always tell a thousand tales and right now I can tell that she's hurting and boy is she hurting bad.

I can't remember seeing her this upset since way back in year ten when her cat died. She bloody loved that crazed, psycho fur-ball. Shame the little shit didn't feel the same way about me. The thing used to make my life hell just for the crack of it. Rachel always thought I was being stupid, but I'm telling you, if that cat could have committed murder, I would have been gone a long time ago.

"Oh no. Please no." I think to myself. If what I'm thinking is true, then this little situation is a whole lot worse that I originally imagined.

"What? Why are you looking at me like that, you weirdo?" She shouts, cutting right into my thoughts.

"Oh my God. It's true, isn't it? You, Rachel, only out for sex and a good time have only gone and done it haven't you?" Rachel doesn't say anything to me, but her eyes grow wide with fear. Yes, I'm bloody right. I know I am. "You've only gone and fallen in love with him."

She still doesn't say anything to me and I take her silence as a big fat yes.

Well, I never thought I'd see the day.

"I don't think I love him." Rachel says after some quiet time. If it's taken this long for her to think about it and then deny it, she most definitely does love him, but she's still in denial. "I think I'm just unsure of these weird feelings that I have when I'm around him."

"You don't believe that for a second. Have you told him?"

"What? Are you stupid? If I'm being honest, I don't think he wants me around anymore. He's been really distant and whenever I do call him, he's always got something on."

"He might just be busy Rach. Why don't you give him a call now?"

"Are you gonna call Matt?" She shoots back at me.

"Fuck off." Why didn't I think that she'd come back with something ridiculous like that?"

The rest of the afternoon passes by slowly. I've got my impending date with Thor looming and I just wish these nerves would do one. They're not welcome here and they need to take a hike and fast. I feel like I've just been on the 'Big One' about five times in a row and every time I move all I want to do is vomit everywhere.

Personally, I've never stepped foot on the 'Big One' and I've not get any intention of doing so in the future, either. But, I'm pretty sure this is exactly how I'd feel if ever I changed my mind. Again, that's highly unlikely. I mean being thrown around a metal cart on a rickety track at only God knows what speed is not my idea of fun. Nope, that shit can be bottled up and saved for the crazy folk. Come on, imagine it breaking down. I can't think of anything worse than plummeting to my death in the middle of a packed-out theme park. Give me the tea-cups any day of the week, oh and if I'm feeling brave then I'll chance the caterpillar too.

As well as my nerves taking over, little miss love machine's been awfully and unusually quiet after our little chat earlier. A part of me feels like I need to call Noah and cancel, but as soon as I mentioned it to Rachel she got her back up and wouldn't hear of it.

"Are you sure you don't want me to stay here?" I ask again, handing Rachel a much needed glass of Prosecco. She takes it like a baby, starving for her elixir of life. "We could binge watch loads of crap T.V and get pissed. We'd have loads of fun."

"Don't be daft. I told you before I'll be fine. Plus, you can't stand him up or drop out at the last minute after he went out of his way to replace your phone."

"Erm, excuse me. I can and I bloody well will. You're more important and you'll always come first, no matter what."

"Piss off, even with a God like creature like him. Jesus Emily, are you blind or something?" She laughs a real, genuine laugh at me and I start to feel better about her staying here alone.

"Always." I reply truthfully, tenderly stroking a stray hair and placing it back behind her ear. "Come on Rach. Please don't make me do this. I don't even know what to say to him."

"You know hello is always a good starting point. Now piss off, go and get ready. Geordie shore's about to start and you know that I'm not prepared to miss this for anyone. Not even you."

Chapter 19

The streets of Camden Town are eerily quiet and it doesn't help ease my anxiety. I love a good busy street at night time. I like to believe that the more people are around you, the less likely you are to be kidnapped or attacked.

However, I do enjoy the peacefulness that comes with it at the same time. Tonight, peace is exactly what I need. Noah, ever the Gentleman that he is offered to pick me up earlier, but I'm a big girl and I hate relying on anyone, especially men.

So, because I'm pretty bloody awesome and Beyoncé's independent woman oozes out of my every pore, I'm now freezing my bloody nips off as I try to find the venue that I'm supposed to be going to. *"Good call Emily, good call."* I give myself a well-deserved mental pat on the back for my efforts. I bet my Mum's so proud of the lady that I've become.

To be honest, I can't even remember the bloody name of the place, so I haven't got a clue where I'm headed. I dig out my phone and scroll to Noah's text to see if I can try and refresh my memory. Nope, it's not there. This could only ever happen to me, for crying out loud. Do I really want to embarrass myself and have to phone him and ask for help? This independence thing is working out fabulously for me so far.

I've only ever been to Camden a handful of times before and that was with Rachel and Mel. When I'm out and about, scouring rails and rails of clothing and must have goodies, why on earth would anyone expect me to take note of my surroundings? Both Rach and Mel are street smart you see, they know places which is pretty awesome for me because all I have to do then is follow their lead.

"You look lost."

I practically jump out of my skin as a tall, dark figure approaches me from the shadows.

"Oh fuck. Not again." I silently scream to myself. Please no. Not here, not now when it's pitch black and I've got absolutely no idea where I'm going.

On instinct, I automatically grab my keys out of my bag for protection. Apparently, it's well known that anything can be used as a weapon if you use your mind. I'm sure that's what The Karate Kid taught us, or maybe that's just what I got from it. I've never really had to put that theory to the test until now.

If this guy even tries the slightest move then I'm going to take everything that I've got, which granted might not be much and gut the prick like a fish.

I stand motionless waiting for him to come closer, but he doesn't, he just stands where he is as if he's been waiting for me. For what though I'm not sure. It's like some crazy scene out of Wild ,Wild West, yet this standoff doesn't really have the same feel to it as we're stood in the middle of the street, in the freezing cold minus any guns and we're in London.

"What do you want?" I ask, my mouth running way ahead of my brain once again. Why do I do it? Why do I always have to open my stupid bloody trap? *Well done Emily, you've just invited this potential weirdo, psycho, lady-killing stranger to enter conversation you muppet. Give yourself another corking pat on the back, you silly cow.*

Strangely he still doesn't say anything and I can't work out his reaction because it's that dark, I can't bloody see him. He's silhouetted right into the darkness. A little bit like a Dementor. To be fair, if it was a Dementor I'm pretty sure I'd be safe because there's not really that much happiness left in my broken, damaged black soul these days.

I look up again and see movement. Oh good, now he's coming closer and I'm that cold I can't bloody move. Maybe I should have put up more of a fight with Rachel. At least that way I would have been at home, tucked up nice and safe right now, instead of walking into the path of death once again.

"Emily, are you okay? It's me." The voice calls out again, only this time I recognise it.

"Noah?" I ask disbelievingly.

"Who else would it be? Are you sure you're okay? You look like you've seen a ghost."

"No, no. I'm fine, you just gave me a little bit of a shock, that's all." I didn't know it was you."

He steps closer and this time I can see him. Really see him, in all his beautiful glory. It must be the light that's caught him at just the right angle because he looks like he's got a halo beaming out of his huge mass of beautiful blonde hair. Thoroughly angelic. "Come on. You look like you're gonna catch your death. You must be freezing. Let's get you inside where it's warm."

What would you know? I don't bloody believe it. The restaurant is right across from where I was stood. Maybe it's about time that I admitted defeat, and my age and finally booked in for that dreaded eye test that I've been putting off for only God knows how long.

Noah's ever the Gentleman, holding the doors, taking my coat and pulling my chair out for me. It's all very swoon-worthy really and I'm just not used to it at all.

Now don't get me wrong, it's all very nice and all but I really don't know how to act. I'll be honest here and admit that I kind of feel a little awkward and that's the last thing that I want to be feeling right now. Maybe Noah's wasting his time on a little old commoner like me. Bloody hell, I'm definitely no lady and this guy clearly deserves one.

"You look beautiful." He smiles over at me once he's taken his seat and I can feel the heat rushing to my cheeks. Crikey, he even compliments too Fortunately, there's a dim glow so I might just get away with it, if not I can always pretend I went a bit over the top with my new NARS Orgasm blush.

"You don't look too bad yourself." I lie. Oh, bloody hell I'm lying all right. He looks gorgeous. He's that hot, I have no doubt in my mind that I could cook my steak on just his flesh alone. I wonder if that's something that he's willing to try? Maybe it's too soon…

He must find my embarrassment highly amusing as he chuckles softly while his sultry eyes never leave mine. I don't even think he blinks. My theory is confirmed... he must be a mythical creature. I just knew it.

"What?" I finally ask, curiosity getting the better of me.

"Nothing." He replies quietly and his hand moves to fill his glass with water, yet he never once looks away from me. Dear God, please don't let this one have some weird random fetish too. I hope I haven't still got the remains of toothpaste around my mush. That'd be attractive, wouldn't it?

I'm getting a little uneasy about the way he's staring at me though. I feel well and truly exposed, like he's got some magical power and he's doing nothing but undressing me with those sinful eyes of his.

Chapter 20

The restaurant is super fancy and the staff are very friendly and welcoming. As I look around, they'd definitely get a five-star rating from me if I was one of those secret shoppers. They look so happy and eager to assist at any given opportunity. They don't seem to be those annoying types just yet. You know the ones, those pesky ones who keeping waltzing over to check everything's okay every five bloody minutes. I hate that. Hate it with a passion and most of the time they start before the food has even arrived. How about asking me once I've taken a bite, pal?

I like to people watch and Noah looks very relaxed and content. Actually, he seems a little bit too happy and relaxed. To top it off, the staff seem to know him on what looks like a rather personal level too.

"So, do you come here often?" I blurt out before I can stop myself. Jeez, this little problem's becoming quite the habit. I'm really curious to know how he came to know these people though. Not that it's any of my business, but I'm a very inquisitive person. I don't think I came across as inquisitive though. No, stupid old me ended up sounding like I was asking the most cheesiest chat-up line of them all.

"Occasionally." Noah smiles while offering me a glass of wine which I dutifully accept, nodding like a wild, sexually deprived loon. He doesn't bother commenting on my weirdness, however. I'm guessing that he's just being polite and there'll be no call back from him for a third date. "I love the food and the atmosphere." He continues as if he can read my mind.

He's not lying. I've yet to try the food, but the atmosphere is definitely rocking. It's quite contagious really.

In all fairness, it's been a hell of a long while since I've been taken out to a restaurant with live music. Actually, it's been a hell of a long time since I've been taken out to a restaurant, full stop. I wonder if most women get treated like this and I was just with a knob for far too long?

"Thanks again for my phone. Really, you shouldn't have." I say, trying my best to change the subject. So what if this is where he brings his dates. Probably a huge fucking queue of dates, but that was all before me. Everyone has a history, some more colourful than others. At the end of the day it's little old me that he's decided to take out tonight, not them. God only knows why, though.

"If I didn't, I don't think that you'd be sat here now, do you?"

Excuse me? Does he think I'm some kind of gold-digger or something? He must notice my expression change as he quickly adds, "it was my way of ensuring that I'd see you again." Oh… "That's why I left my number in the phone. That way it was entirely up to you if you deleted it or decided to take it further. Luckily for me, here you are.

"Oh shit. Holy mother of Jesus." I cry out, disbelief and agony rippling through my entire body and morphing into one. I don't bloody believe this. I only planned to nip to the little ladies room for a quick pee and to powder my nose and now I wish that I hadn't have even bothered.

What the hell am I supposed to do now? I can't go out there like this. For God sake, I wont even be able to walk unless I go commando. Then Noah will think I'm gagging for it and I'm an easy lay. Yes, I'm human and I'd be lying if I said I didn't have a teeny, tiny feeling in my knickers, or at least I did before this horrific pain kicked in. Now that feeling has gone and has been replaced by a pure, intense inferno.

"Have a wax." Rachel said.

"Go on, you may as well." She said.

"Sex is a hell of a lot more intense with the wig ripped off." She said.

I bloody knew that I shouldn't have listened to her. *Always follow your gut Emily.* That's what my Mum always said. But did I? Did I bloody buggeries.

Now, because of my own stupid and indecisive recklessness, even knowing how sensitive my skin is, because I stupidly went against my gut instinct and gave into peer pressure and had the thing whipped off; now I've got what feels like horrific and agonising third degree burns all over my poor Vajayjay.

That definitely throws the sex right out the window. Not that there would have been any, anyway, but what with my unpredictable behaviour at the minute, it's really hard to say for certain. My nymphomaniac side could erupt at any moment.

My God, it's angry looking. All red, inflamed and full of what looks like blisters. Anyone would think that I've contracted herpes or something similar.

My heart stops... Shit.

Matt... Matt's the only person that I've slept with in over a year. That's twelve whole months and now I'm breaking out with something unpleasant. What if Matt's given me genital fucking herpes? You can't get rid of the bastards once you've caught them. I know that much. They just keep coming back for more and more.

After I've finally pulled my knickers back up, I try to slowly move my right leg in front of the other but it hurts too much. The pain is unbearable. Sweet Jesus, child birth is probably an absolute breeze compared to this throbbing festation. I try again and give up just as fast. I'm really left with no other choice here. I'm going to have to go commando and quickly come up with the mother of all excuses to get out of here and get home as quickly as possible.

Digging deep in my bag for what feels like the tenth time tonight, I pull out my phone and quickly type out *'S.O.S. URGENT, I repeat, URGENT S.O.S.'* and send it to Rachel. All I can do now is hope and pray that she's still awake and hasn't fallen into a Prosecco and chocolate induced coma. If she has then I'm well and truly up shit street.

It must easily take a good fifteen minutes to finally emerge from the ladies and with each step that I take my eyes are watering more and more with the pain. As for silver linings, at least this mascara has stood the test of time and lived up to its waterproof claims. It bloody should do for the price too.

"Are you okay?" Noah asks as I slowly ease myself down into my chair, praying that he can't tell that there's something wrong. Something majorly wrong. Why does nothing ever go right for me? Why does there always have to be some drama along the way? "You had me worried for a while there. I thought you'd called for back-up and fled the scene."

"If only you knew what was really happening." I think, but instead say, "no, no. Just topping up the face." I hate lying and I can't believe I'm lying to him already, but does he really need to know about my horrific fanny rash? I never even made it to the make-up part and now I'm quickly blistering away as I not so patiently wait for my back-up to hurry up and bloody help me out of this pickle that I'm in, once again thanks to her.

I look back up at Noah and smile as hard as I can. I don't want him to know that something's wrong, but at the same time I also don't want to look to eager either.

Well this is a flaming bag of shit isn't it? Dating and me really don't go hand in hand. First my phone, ultimate love of my life breaks and now I'm sat here practically starkers and my foof looks riddled. I really hope that it isn't. I must be a really terrible person. I go off the rails once and this is what happens. Jesus, Mary and Joseph, I'm turning out to be the type of girl that Mum's all over the world warn their sons about.

I feel like crying, but I can't because the Noah will know something is up and if I start crying now then I won't be able to stop. *Bloody hell Emily, how could you be so stupid.* Wax or no wax, I've possibly just ruined my whole future for one stupid, yet highly pleasant drunken fumble.

Matt... I swear to God when I finally see him, I'm going to squeeze his balls so tight that he's going to wish that he was born a woman.

My phone rings just in time, right before an awkward silence on my part can settle in between us. "Sorry." I say. "I forgot to switch it to silent. I'm not normally so rude. "I'm genuinely sorry for all of this. I feel absolutely shocking about this whole situation, but what can I do? I'm a mess, my vagina's a mess and I really need to get home. To feel some sense of normality and security again.

I quickly glance at the screen and feign a shocked expression as I see Rachel's name flickering before me. "I really need to get this." I lie again.

Noah nods while topping up our glasses. I really wish he wasn't so nice and polite. I'd feel less of a bitch that way.

"Hello." I say as soon as I answer.

"This better be freaking good." Rachel hisses down the line at me, clearly pissed that I've come between her and her Geordie Shore catch-up.

"Oh my God, that's terrible. Are you okay? You really shouldn't be on your own." I press the volume keys down on the side of my phone just in case she breaks out into a major hissy fit. There's just no telling with her sometimes. Best to be prepared for every possible opportunity.

"I'll give you terrible if this is just your nerves talking."

"No." I answer her question, but place my hand over my mouth for added effect on Noah's part. "No, of course I'll be there. Give me half an hour, maybe an hour tops."

I shut the phone off and catch Noah watching me closely. "Is everything okay?" He asks, ever the Gentleman.

"I really wish I could say that it was." I say glumly and I'm not exactly lying. Everything's not okay and it feels like it's getting worse by the minute. I guess it can't help sitting down on it and adding pressure to my already swollen lady parts. "I hate to do this Noah. I feel terrible, really I do, but I have to go. Rachel's had some bad news and there's no way that I can leave her on her own at a time like this."

"Is she okay? Is there anything that I can do?" He asks, genuinely concerned.

Well, if you can stop my Vajayjay from feeling like it's the hot spot of hell, then yes. I don't voice this out loud though, instead I say, "I'm not too sure right now. I think she'd like to keep it private for now. I hope you don't mind? Honestly, this really couldn't have happened at a more inconvenient time." Again I'm being truthful here, it's just that Noah has no idea what I'm really going on about.

"No, no. Not at all. You go and be with your friend. She clearly needs you and we can always do this again another time?"

"That sounds good to me." Bloody hell, why does he have to be so nice and understanding? I didn't think it was possible for men like him to exist. Rachel always warned me about them, but I was adamant it wasn't possible and that they were all mythical creatures. There's no way that I deserve to be going on dates with someone like him. He's just too perfect. I'm really not used to it and it just shocks me at every turn.

"How will you get back? Would you like me to come with you?" Yes I would. I'd love to take him with me and hide him away and keep him all to myself forever. But if he takes one look at my fanny, then he'll run a mile. "It's pretty dark out there and I kind of hate the idea of you getting the tube on your own." See what I mean? Tyler would have just left me to it, without so much as a second thought until he stumbled home and felt like a little poke in the middle of the night.

"No, I'll be okay. I'll get a cab. I hate the tube at night too." It always reminds me of that one scene in Ghost. Every time a can flies past me, I'm stood wondering if it's the wind or if someone's actually silently watching me from the shadows.

"Right, well if you're sure? But please let me pay. No…" he holds his big strong hands up to stop my protests and sternly says, "I insist and there won't be any arguments about it."

"Way to go Emily, well done. You're ditching this guy all because one way or another, you just couldn't keep your legs closed. You need to hurry up and sort your shit out and get your bloody priorities straight before you end up all wrinkly and lonely."

"Thank you." I finally manage to say after winning the war of words in my head. Once again I feel like a right ungrateful bitch, slightly horrific at the person that I'm fast becoming and I'm sore, so, so unbelievably sore.

Chapter 21

"Have you seen the state of this?" I shout out to Rachel as soon as I hobble into my front room, only to find her in exactly the same spot that I left her in right in front of the T.V. Do you know, I could have really needed her tonight and would she have cared? Would she hell.

Her head finally spins around to face me and she doesn't look happy. Not in the slightest. "What, the moron stood before me who's too scared to go out on a date and has to find any excuse to come running home?" Wow. Her reactions a little more harsh than I anticipated.

Oh how the high and mighty will mock me, but right now I'm in too much pain to care.

"No this." I slowly hobble towards her so that she can see all of me and without so much as a second thought, I hastily pull my dress up over my waist and flash her my lady parts in all their horrific, swollen glory. Well, it's nothing that she hasn't already seen before. We're best friends, we know everything that there is to know about each other, including body parts.

"Shitting hell Emily, that looks painful." Rachel shouts as she takes in a full eyeful of my swollen lips and jumps from the couch to get a closer inspection. "What is it?" She cries out. I don't know whether I need to start panicking now or not as she looks genuinely concerned and that really scares me. Rachel knows everything and she only ever looks worried if she has reason too.

"How the hell do I know?" If I knew I wouldn't be going out of my flaming mind with worry, would I? "I just went to the ladies and bam, this massive infestation has taken over my foof."

"Have you tried to put anything on it?"

"Like what? Cleary I just wander around carrying lotions and potions for this kind of thing." I reply sarcastically. "Come on Rach, don't be a tit."

"Don't be a bloody bitch." She quips right back.

Don't be a bitch? I'm fucking in agony here. I've got every bloody right to be a bitch.

"We need to put something on this and fast."

No shit. Here I was not so patiently enjoying the pain and waiting for it to spread. "You can't touch it though. What if you catch it?" I don't want to be the one who accidently riddles Rachel too.

"Emily, I highly doubt that a bad reaction is contagious."

"No you're right. But genital herpes is rife. "I exclaim and Rachel pauses in the hallway before turning back to look at me. I'm not too sure that I like the expression on her face right now though. It's not a very nice look. More of a 'why am I best friends with a daft bint' look.

"You've not got genital herpes you daft mare. That's a reaction to the wax you had earlier."

"Oh, so this is all your fault then?" I ask.

"No, you can't blame your ridiculous sensitive skin on me. Plus, I tend to get it from time to time, just never this severe. I can't even begin to imagine how painful it is. But, now that I've had a closer look I can promise you that you'll be fine in no time."

Not herpes? Well, that's bloody music to my ears, that is. "So what do I do to make it better?"

"All you need is a nice cool bath and then make sure that you slap loads of this on and I mean go real heavy with the shit. Plus, the cooling sensation will give you some relief, but try not to scratch the itch." She hurries back towards me from the kitchen and hands me a grey tub.

"Sudacrem?" I take it and silently thank her for being the sensible one and always ensuring that my first aid kit is thoroughly stocked and ready to go.

"Yes. Sudacrem, you know the baby nappy rash cream? It'll work wonders, plus it's got antibacterial properties in it too so you'll be less likely to get any nasty infections around it. Just think, your front bum will be all silky and smooth in no time, too. Now, if you don't mind,

Gary and co are waiting for me to take them off pause. You know how I don't like to keep them waiting."

"Oh no, don't you worry about me, I'll be perfectly fine. You happily go off and pretend to be one of those Worldies, or whatever they like to call themselves."

"Oh, don't you worry your pretty little head. I fully intend too." She claps her hands excitedly before settling herself back down again. "Ten out of ten for getting out of the sex though. That shit beats your usual 'I'm on my period' excuse hands down."

"Don't be jealous now. Green doesn't suit you."

"Ha, jealous I am not. However, had you actually don't the deed and shagged him senseless like he very much deserves, now that would be a completely different matter."

"Yeah, yeah, whatever." I mutter as I slowly and very carefully walk up the stairs. Oh, sod it. Maybe crawling would be better?

Note to self, stick to shaving. Waxing is the Devil; the root of all evil.

Chapter 22

"How you feeling now?"

Rachel's delicate tones greet me as I hobble into the front room. "Sore." I reply truthfully. As much as I wanted to, I never managed to make it back downstairs again last night after my bath. It was that soothing that I didn't want to move, frightened that if I did then it would set the pain off again. Yet, weirdly my common sense decided to make an appearance and kicked in, reminding me that I'd probably be worse off if I got hypothermia. To tell you the truth, it wouldn't be all that surprising really, I seem to be getting my right fair share of everything else; or so it seems.

"There's fresh coffee in the pot if you want some?"

"Is the pope a catholic?" I ask and Rachel just rolls her eyes at my sarcasm. "I don't mean to be rude, but what are you still doing here, anyway? I thought you would have been up, dressed and already at work by now?"

"Well I would have been, but someone decided it would be a great idea to be a lazy cow and crawled out of bed late."

I look over to my best friend and wonder for a moment as to whether she actually has any brain cells left in that pretty little head of hers. "Sorry to disappoint, but in case you forgot, I don't really have anything to get up for right now."

"See, now that's where you're wrong." She stands up and the walks towards me with a really serious look on her face. Not today. I really can't be doing with one of her lectures. I'd rather endure a major hangover than deal with the bullshit that's about to come from her mouth. I love her and all, but sometimes she's just too much for me to handle. However, seeing as though I've lost some of my mobility and speed, there's no way that I'll be able to get away from her fast enough, so I'll just have to endure it.

"Rach, if you're going to start preaching at me, make it quick and please, for the love of God let me have my coffee first."

"Oh, I'll be super quick about it, don't you worry about that. Plus, if anything, you'll need to be quick at getting ready once I've filled you in on all the details."

My eyes rise to meet hers, no matter how much I try to stop them. What the hell is she bloody harping on about? "Okay, I'm lost. Come on Rach, don't talk in riddles. Help a girl out, at least." I half plead with her while grabbing my coffee mug and preparing myself for what could be an overly long and cryptic speech.

My eyes remain fixed on Rachel as I silently observe her. Rachel looks pretty nervous about something which isn't like her at all. You can tell that she desperately wants to tell me something, but she doesn't know how, or where to start. "Okay, before I start promise me you won't get mad?"

"So I'm obviously going to get mad if you start with something like that."

"Yes, probably. Maybe? Either way I just know that in the end you'll be really happy and grateful that I did what I did though."

"Did what? Flaming hell. You're not making any sense." What the hell have I come down to here? I should have just stayed in bed. I'd probably get more sense out of my quilt at this rate. "Please just hurry up and tell me what you need to tell me. I'm still sore and my brains still half asleep."

"Well..." She shifts slowly from foot to foot and she can't even look me in the eye. "Erm, okay... well, when you were out last night I thought I'd have a little whip around, you know to help you out a bit and then that's one less thing for you to worry about..."

"Okay... thanks." I say gratefully. Rachel knows that I absolutely detest cleaning with a passion. I can't tell you how many times I've contemplated hiring out a cleaner. Lazy I know, but I'm not afraid to admit that I have zero shame, none whatsoever and there are much more exciting things that I could be doing with my time, or at least there were.

"I noticed a pile of post just shoved to the side, so I walked away because well, that's your personal stuff and I'd never intrude you know that..." she pauses and bites down nervously on her lower lip.

"Well no you shouldn't have been snooping, you're right there. But, I'm going to take a wild guess and say that you went right ahead and opened them all up anyway and had yourself a right good nosey?" Fortunately for me, we don't really tend to keep things from each other, otherwise this could end up turning out pretty embarrassing. But, I don't have anything to hide. Unless she's stumbled across my most recent credit card bill. Do you know I actually think that's due to arrive any day now, too? If it is my credit card bill that she's harping on about then I just know that I'm about to get the grilling of a lifetime. If there's one thing that gets Rachel's back up, it's debt and reckless spending. Well, that's two but you get my point.

"I'm sorry." She continues, without so much as giving my impending heart attack so much as a second thought. "I tried to leave them alone, really I did, but every time I walked away I had a nagging feeling that there was something really important hidden in there."

"And was there? I wouldn't really count the gas and electricity statements as important, Rach."

"It's not that, it's…" She says and then goes quiet again. I know she doesn't mean to, but she's really starting to get on my tits a little.

"For crying out loud." I shout. I can't take much more of this. She's driving me insane going all around the houses like this. "Just tell me what it was." She flinches back a little and she looks like I've just physically slapped her across the face. "Oh Rach, I'm sorry. I've hardly woken up and you're chucking all this shit on me and won't get to the bloody point." I'm not a morning person, never have been and most probably never will be.

"No, no, it's fine. I should be the one saying sorry, but at the same time I'm not sorry." She draws in a deep breath and then quickly says, "It's about your suspension meeting with H.R. It's this afternoon."

I'm frozen to the spot, fear rippling through my entire body, and I'm absolutely petrified of the unknown. "Well that was bloody quick, wasn't it?" I say out loud and to no one in particular.

"Surely that has to be a good thing?" Rachel smiles back at me, but it's not a full, confident smile.

"It does? How do you work that out then? None of this is good Rach. None of this should even be happening in the first place."

"I know, but surely if they've inspected everything and checked through all of their so-called evidence this quickly, then they mustn't have anything on you. Hey, you never said if Mel got back to you the other day, has she heard anything?"

"Shit. I completely forgot to send her my new number. Even if she has text me there's no way that I'll be able to read it as my screens too far gone." I know my heads been all over the place, but how could I forget to send her my new number?

"I'm sure she'll get in touch soon enough. Plus, you need to think positive right now. Hopefully once you've been in, you'll be back in the office without so much as another word said about it." That's Rachel, always trying to find the best in every possible situation. I wish I felt the same.

"Oh, they'll be words all right and lots of them. But first I want to know what I've supposedly done to deserve all this bullshit."

"And you will, but right now you need to head up those stairs and get a wriggle on because it starts at two o'clock."

I chance a quick look at the clock next to the tele and see that it's almost twelve. I shouldn't be all that surprised really, nothing's ever simple with me at all.

Chapter 23

I arrive outside the office with around five minutes to spare. "Talk about cutting it finely." I whisper to Rachel. I have never rushed upstairs, showered, and got dressed as fast as I did before for as long as I can remember.

"You're here now and you're not late. That's all that matters." She gives my weak, limp and lifeless body a quick squeeze of encouragement, but I still feel numb.

This is it. It's all real and sooner or later I'm going to find out my fate. "Come on, let's go and give them what for."

I really wish I had Rachel's fiery attitude right now. But I don't. Instead, I feel, well in all honesty I don't know what I feel, but it's definitely not me. Hopefully something will spark in me when I get inside the meeting, otherwise I'm going to be buggered. "After you." Is all I can just about manage and I plaster on a really fake smile for Rachel's sake. She'd kick my arse if she knew just how nervous I am. I don't even know why because it's not like I've got anything to prove to anyone, least of all Graham, because I haven't done anything wrong. I'm one hundred percent sure of it.

It feels weird to be walking into the building that I have spent most of my adult life, only to get out on a completely different floor. In all the years that I've worked here, never have I once had an incident where I've needed to go up to H.R's floor. I always thought that was a pretty good thing, but today, here I am.

As soon as the lift doors open, I find myself stood face to face with Graham. "Hi" I say with a smile, hoping that this time he might just be on my side. But boy am I wrong. He doesn't even smile back, just gives me a quick nod and stands to the side so that I can exit the lift. What has gotten in to him? I try again to speak to him, but really I don't know why I'm bothering. Rachel must sense my sudden discomfort as her hand clasps around mine and she tightens hers encouragingly; silently telling me that I've got this. I breathe in and then find the balls to speak again. "Are you not going to be in the meeting?"

Graham just stares right above my head, point blank refusing to make eye contact with me like I've been a really naughty little girl and I've disappointed him beyond all reason. After a while, he replies with a flat "yes" and his jaw is clenched. Am I that much of a horrible person?

"Okay, well I guess I'll see you in there, then." It's like I've been abandoned; disowned. All for something that I don't bloody know about. I'd undoubtedly have more chance of getting blood from a stone than getting him to let me in on what's actually happened. It's so unfair.

Without another word, he steps inside the lift and I watch as the doors slowly close behind him.

"I thought he just said he was going to be at the meeting?" Rachel's voice pulls me back to where I am and I'd love to be anywhere but here.

"He did. Maybe he's left something that he needs?" She shrugs back at and she smiles encouragingly.

"Yeah, his balls and his common bloody sense."

"Emily, if you'd like to come on through?" A small, middle aged blonde lady appears from one of the side doors and looks at me pitifully. Well, that in itself tells me that this whole meeting is bad. Very bad.

I nod back at her, pretending that I'm fine; that all this will be some huge messed up mistake and I'll be back at my desk downstairs in a matter of minutes, just like Rachel said earlier. Pursing my lips together I smooth down my pencil skirt and do my best to hold my head high as I walk through the dark oak fire doors.

The large room is intimidating. Especially the two strangers who are sat before me. Yes, they may smile at me, but that's just being polite and it's totally part of their job. God forbid if they're evil to anyone, then they'd find themselves sat on the opposite end of the table.

"Emily, I'm Stacey, head of Human resources and this is Neil, he'll be scribing for us today." It's such a shame that this is happening, because she really does look like someone who I could natter to over a coffee in the staff room. Neil on the other hand looks bored shitless and would rather claw his eyeballs out than have to sit here and scribe for God knows how long. "We'll get started as soon as Graham comes back, okay?"

"You know I shouldn't even be here. I haven't done anything wrong." I protest, but I know that it's fallen on deaf ears straight away. I bet they hear this type of thing all the time, a bit like a judge in a courtroom. Bloody hell, if that's the case then it looks like morbid Neil is my jury. I may as well take my lazy fat arse out of this chair and head home now. Stacey on the other hand just about manages to give me that pitiful smile again.

Let's face it. I'm fucked and there's nothing that I can do about it apart from endure this pointless meeting. Everyone's clearly already made their minds up about this whole little pickle that I'm in.

Graham finally makes an appearance after ten awfully long minutes. The tension in the room is horrible, even Rachel seems uncomfortable and she's usually fine in any situation. Yet instead, all she can do is nervously fiddle with her perfectly manicured nails. I've got no idea where she finds the time to keep herself so pristine all the time. Maybe she could give me some pointers so I no longer look homeless.

"It's not looking all that good, is it?" I whisper to her.

"Just keep your chin up and stay positive. Make sure you stand your ground too. Don't let them intimidate you." Her voice quivers as she rushes the words out. Great, how am I supposed to stay positive when my partner in crime knows fully well that all's lost?

I've got no idea why, but I try to make eye contact with Graham again when he takes his seat. I shouldn't be all too surprised when he refuses to look at me again. I never took him for a coward, but then you always learn something new about people every day.

"Okay, now that Graham's here we can start." Stacey says, shuffling a stack of papers in her hands. Neil on the other hand looks like he'd rather throw himself off this building, either that or he's got his resting bitch face mastered to a tee.

"I take it you know why we're here today, Emily?" She starts.

"Actually no. No I don't and I'm kind of looking forward to finding out." I say, before she can continue. My eyes burn into Graham as I say this, but again he seems to be too busy to look at me. *"Come on,"* I want to shout. Graham could pull this back if he wanted too. Why isn't he stopping this mahoosive pile of ridiculous crap?

Stacey looks at me before turning her attention to my once perfect boss and he shrugs, "I sent all the relevant paperwork out. All protocols were followed from this end."

He did? I sure as hell didn't receive anything. I turn to Rachel and she gives me a glum look that I interpret to mean, *"I didn't get around to opening all your post."* "I'd just like to say in my defence that I haven't received anything other than a letter regarding this meeting today." If anything, I have to get my side across here.

"Well, I have a copy of everything that has been sent and documented so we can go over it all, that's not a problem."

I want to say so much, to tell them how unfair all of this is, but my gut's telling me that none of it will help my case so I bite down on my lip to prevent the words from breaking free.

"It seems that there have been some serious allegations made against you Emily. We have a range of things here from misuse of the company's internet policy, also fraudulent claims against the business' expenses account and finally sexual harassment."

"Excuse me?" I shout out, struggling to hold my tongue any further. "Did you just say fraud and sexual harassment? Graham, what's actually going on here?" I demand even though I know it's in vain.

"As soon as the allegations were brought to my attention I looked into it further." Again, he's looking over me, not at me and it's driving me insane. Where are your balls, goddamn it? "I had I.T. look into the claims for misuse and all of your internet history and I was shocked at what came back to me Emily."

"We have some picture evidence here if you'd like to see it?"

"Yes." Picture evidence? This is absolute bullshit. I take the papers from Stacey and quickly riffle through them. What's before me is horrifying. Not only does it show that I have been ordering a shed load of goodies from the business account, there's numerous screenshots from conversations between me and random guys on bloody dating sites. Oh god, oh no... there's images too. Naked ones. "You've got this all wrong." I plead. "I haven't done this. Why would I do any of this from work? If I was into this kind of thing, which I'm not, I'd make sure that I did it from the privacy of my own home."

"Are you sure that it wasn't you?" Stacey asks, squinting slightly as if she can see the lies seeping out of me.

"I'm one hundred percent sure." I reply confidently.

"You know there was a time that I would have believed you." Graham looks at me, actually looks me right in the eye, but his face doesn't look friendly at all. He looks like I'm something that's just crawled through an open window and he can't wait to squash me. "However, if you look at the bottom of each page, it clearly shows your user I.D and then there are the emails that have come straight from your mailbox."

"But…"

"I'd like to think after all the years that we've worked together, you'll finally give me the truth?"

"I am. I didn't do it Graham. You know this isn't something that I would do. I work hard and I always have. I'm the one who has always carried everyone else in this place and I didn't mind one bit, because I loved my job. I bloody loved the people that I worked with. We we're supposed to be some kind of happy family, but I guess it looks like you're happy to pick and choose who fits and who doesn't."

"Like I said Emily, it's out of my hands. As you can see, it's all here in black and white. To say that I'm beyond upset and disappointed is an understatement. You were, and have always been my best and most loyal employee and there was never a doubt in my mind that I could always trust and rely on you."

"What? You still can. This all has to be some messed up joke. It's completely out of character for me. Can't you see that this has to be some kind of set up."

"Do you have reason to believe that anyone would want to set you up?" Stacey asks.

Cruella automatically comes to the forefront of my mind. Yes, we don't like each other very much, that's no secret, but would she really go out of her way to destroy me like that? I don't think so. It all sounds like too much effort on her part and we all know that she likes to spend all of her time on herself. "Graham..." I say again, but he looks beyond angry now.

"I'm in shock that you would actually go out of your way to violate our reputation like that. I've always liked to treat you all fair, so what have I done to make you repay me like this?"

"For God sake." I snap, tears of frustration threatening to break free at any minute. One thing that I will not do is cry in front of these people. I'm being backed into a corner and it's not fair at all. I turn my head to Rachel to see what she's thinking throughout all of this, but all she does is squeeze my hand gently. "I didn't do it." I say again, but now I'm the one who can't look anyone in the eye. Not because I'm a coward, but because I can't believe that no one is listening to me.

"Here, get this down you."

"I feel physically sick Rach." I take the cup from her hand and look at it disapprovingly.

"We'll get you something stronger later. We don't want you having drunk and disorderly adding to that ridiculous list, do we?"

Ridiculous is one word for it. While we're out here, tweedle-dee, tweedled-dum and nasty Neil are currently sat inside that little room discussing my fate. How could all of this have happened? "I'm done for Rach." I say out loud and now it feels real. I'm going to be jobless any second and there is nothing that I can do about it. I don't want to have to work with Rachel. I love her and all, but that is something that would really test our friendship. I know that I'm lucky to have her to fall back on, but if I can keep my rightful job here, a job that I love, then that's what I'm going to do.

"Do you really think it was a set up?" Rachel asks me, and takes the chair opposite mine.

"I don't know. It has to be something like that, because I sure as hell haven't done anything on that list. Yes, every now and again I'll have a quick nosey on

Twitter and Facebook, but that's all done in my lunch hour, which is allowed. It says that the internet can be used for personal use outside of office hours in our contracts."

"I know, I believe you." She says gently and her hand wraps around mine again.

"Well at least someone does. Did you see how they were coming at me like vultures? It didn't matter what I said, they just weren't listening. Their minds have been made up from day one on this."

"You know what they say Emily, it's not over until the fat lady sings. Keep that pretty little chin up and held high." Just as Rachel finishes talking, the door swings open and Stacey calls me back in.

I've never been so scared in all my life.

Chapter 24

What a day.

Nothing could have prepared me for what I faced when I walked back inside that little meeting room. Stacey was as empathetic as one can be in that kind of situation, Graham looked defeated, and slightly broken somehow and Neil, fucking hell it was the first time that I actually saw him crack a smile, full of relief that his strenuous task was finally over. I've honestly never met anyone as obnoxious as he was. Honestly, the guy needs to take a long look in the mirror and have a serious talk with himself.

At least I wanted to keep my job. He couldn't give ten bloody hoots as to whether he was there or not. Life's a cruel bitch sometimes. I definitely learned that today, right when I was dismissed on the spot without so much as a word from Graham. I'm really annoyed how he was harping on about how I let him down. *"No sunshine, hopefully one day when you wake up and realise that this was all some massive error, maybe you'll stop and see how much you have let me down."*

Rachel wanted to come back with me, but I left her in town, forcing her to contact Doug and spend some time with him. When we stepped outside, he'd blown her phone up with at least thirty missed calls. Obviously, Rachel being Rachel, she was just going to ignore him, but there was no way that I could just stand back and allow that to happen. No way. "What good will that do the two of you?" I pointed out to her. "He seems pretty keen to talk to you if you ask me. Go and call him. You might just live to regret it if you don't. Trust me, I'll be okay." I lied. I felt horrible doing it, but it was the only way that I could get her off my back. As much as I love her, having her fussing over me would only make me feel worse.

"Are you sure?" She looks so unsure as she asks me this, but I have to stay strong here. She really needs to sort things out with her shag partner and I really need some alone time while I try and get my head together.

"Of course, there's a bottle of wine or three with my name on at the corner shop which I fully intend to get down and personal with." She wasn't happy, but I was adamant. All I wanted was to be alone so that I could cry in my own little bubble, with no distractions. "I'll call you later." I promised, and off she went, reluctantly to finally sort things out with Doug.

Now, all alone in my house, nursing my wine, I'm not too sure it was a good idea to be left alone with my thoughts. Especially when you throw alcohol in to the mix. I'm still in shock. It doesn't seem real that I have just been sacked. Never in my whole working life have I ever been sacked, but today as soon as I stepped back inside that room, they dismissed me on the spot. I tried to argue, to plea my case, but it was pretty clear that their minds were already made up; Graham's included. I wouldn't be all that surprised if the final decision was down to him too.

Now here I'm sat at my kitchen table like a sad, depressed loner. Maybe it's time that I woke up and realised that this is now me, now my life and I'm just going to have to deal with it. I'm going to have to find some way of adjusting. Bloody hell, I'm almost thirty and I've got absolutely nothing to show for it. What have I done with my life? Everything that I once had, has now disappeared in to thin air. My boyfriend didn't want me anymore, and now the company that I loved to work for doesn't want me either.

"At least you'll never leave me. You'll always need me, won't you?" I ask the bottle of wine in front of me, and I'd like to think that it just shimmied its contents at me in agreement.

As I lift up the bottle to refill my glass, I notice Tyler's package still on the table where I left it. Honestly, I don't know why I haven't just thrown it in the bin. It's not doing anything for me by reminding me of him. Instead, all it's doing is reminding me of what I once had.

Thinking about it, I'm pretty surprised that Rachel didn't go snooping through it after she started riffling through my post. On closer inspection, it doesn't look like it's been tampered with and if she has then she clearly didn't think its contents were important enough to tell me about.

"Oh Tyler, why after all this time are you still trying to tear me apart." I sway a little as I stand, a little lightheaded from the wine and my empty stomach and lean forward to grab the package ready to throw whatever it is in the bin where it belongs. I lift my arm up, just about to let go when curiosity gets the better of me. Maybe I could have a little peak. I wouldn't want a whole bunch of what-if's flying around inside my head in months to come. Plus, I'm pretty sure whatever is inside can't make me feel worse than I already do right now.

Wrong. Oh, how wrong…

I couldn't have been more wrong if I'd tried. My hands tremble as I look inside the box. What is this? Some sick joke? Why would he do this to me now after all this time? No phone calls, no apologies. Bloody hell, not even a single explanation for why he messed up our relationship and everything that we could have had, all because he thought it was a great idea to mess it all up to please his sad and selfish needs. Deep down, I always knew he was a prick, but at a certain time in my life he was my prick and I loved him. Jesus, as much as I hate him, absolutely detest him, I guess a part of me will always love him. As much as I don't want to, there's not much that I can do about it. He was my first love and my first heartbreak.

A huge burst of anger overcomes me and all I can see is red. I don't know if it's purely because of Tyler's gift, or a multitude of everything that has happened recently finally coming to a head and taking its toll, but I feel like hulk smashing the shit out of everything in sight. Instead, I throw his stupid bloody package to the floor and a piece of paper falls out and lands on the table before me.

"Great, as if the gift wasn't insult enough, he now feels the need to explain something to me after almost a year." I always assumed that he was off living the dream with Suzy the bloody floozy. Cleary she could do everything that I couldn't and what I could do, she must have been able to do it better.

Oh what the hell, I'm a glutton for punishment anyway so I may as well see what he's got to say for himself. No doubt he's loving life, living in a perfect family home whilst she's busy making homemade goodies, heavily pregnant about to make their life complete.

To calm myself, I take a big glug of wine and sit back down. Jesus, he could have at least put some effort into his handwriting. If you want to tell someone something, then for the love of everything that is holy, please make it legible.

Emily,

You're probably surprised to hear from me to say the least, but I've been meaning to do this for a long time. I guess I just never had the balls to put pen to paper. I can imagine what's going on in your head right now, you huffing like you always do when you don't agree with me, and yes, you're right I've never really had any balls to begin with.

I hope you're well and you've managed to get over what I did to you, to us. I never, ever meant to hurt you. That was never part of the plan. None of this was part of the plan.

I'm sure you'll agree that things hadn't been great for us for quite a while, and I know that's no excuse for my actions. You'll never really understand how sorry I am.

Our life was supposed to be great. We were supposed to grow old together. But that will never happen now and I'm finally man enough to take whole responsibility for that.

I want you to know that if I could go back in time and erase the massive fuck up that I caused, I would. I'd do it in a heartbeat. Without a doubt.

Maybe I should have stayed and tried to talk it out with you, to try and make you understand. I was lost Emily, really lost. I thought that I had already lost you and you didn't care about us anymore. My head was all over the place. Thoughts were going through my mind that I shouldn't have even been thinking about.

Anyway, that's the past and what's done is done, regrettably.

I've always loved you and I think I always will. My life's not been the same since I made that terrible mistake. I bet you're sat at the kitchen table now, looking cute with that confused look on your face. I would be too.

The ring... Well, I'd bought it a few months prior to the shit hitting the fan. What with my promotion, I could finally get down on one knee and ask you to be my wife. Maybe I should have been stronger. Maybe I should have tried to talk to you more instead of shutting you out. Hell, I should have done a lot of things differently.

I doubt that you'll keep it and I don't blame you. But it doesn't feel right me keeping it. I bought it for you and it's you that should have it. I'll understand if you throw it, but I'll feel better knowing that I finally gave it to you. It felt wrong that I had kept on to it.

I'm so sorry that I hurt you. I'll never forgive myself for breaking your heart, it's something that I will carry with me for as long as I live, but it has taught me to really appreciate what you have and to never take anything for granted.

I don't have a right to miss you, but I do. I don't have a right to love you but I do and I will do, always.

I hope life treats you kind Emily, because there is no one in the world who deserves it more.

You'll be forever in my heart.

T x

I re-read his letter a dozen times, over and over until I can't see any more from the onslaught of tears that are breaking through. Talk about a head fuck. Why would I want to know all that now? What could I possibly gain from it, closure? I've spent months upon months trying to pick myself back up again and now he's just undone everything with a poxy ring and some meaningless words on a letter. Today can go and suck donkey balls. Maybe it's best if I just go to bed and hope for better tomorrow.

Just as I'm about to listen to my own advice for a change, my phone buzzes to life beside me. I look down and see Rachel's name flashing up on the screen. As much as I'd rather not speak to anyone right now and just wallow in my own self-pity, I can't ignore her. I owe it to her to answer. I've shut her out too much already. Throughout all of this Rachel has been my rock. She's the one who constantly picks me up when times get tough and she's the first to give me a good old kick up the arse when it's needed too. Even if I don't agree with her at the time, I know she's doing what's right for me. As much as my selfish side wants too, there's just no way that I can shut her out now.

"Hello." I say when I answer and as much as I try to prevent it, my voice betrays me by quivering and my bottom lip won't stop shaking. My, now the dams are well and truly open.

"Hey, what's wrong? Are you crying?" She asks, concern thick in her tone. There's no way that I'm going to be able to get out of this one. Not now, not after today and my wine consumption, I'm too far gone to lie. I just don't have the energy left in me.

"Uhh-hhh."

"I'll be right over."

I don't get a chance to blubber anything else out before the call disconnects. Now she's going to be hot on her heels to see me. Shit. I should have pretended to be okay. What if I've gone and ruined something between her and Doug? I don't want to get in the middle of those two because I know if they both work on it and start to be open and honest with each other then they'll have something special. I just know it. Plus, I'm morbid enough already for the both of us. I guess there's nothing really left for me to do apart from cry and finish this bottle off before she gets here.

Chapter 25

"What do you mean? You're not making any sense Emily."

Rachel arrived about fifteen minutes ago and since she got here she's been trying to find out what's happened to make me so upset. I tried to tell her, but the words just wouldn't come and I ended up getting myself that worked up that I could feel a bloody panic attack coming on.

This isn't good. None of this is good. "Tyler..." I finally manage to say his name without choking on it.

"Please tell me he hasn't decided to just turn up after all this time?" I shake my head, unable to go into it all just now. I'm only just starting to get my breathing back under control and I don't fancy getting that worked up again. Instead of talking, I somehow find the strength within me to pick his letter up and pass it to her.

"Is this what was in the package?" Just one look at her face and I can tell that she's seething. It's a shame that he isn't here because I know just from her reaction that she'd do her bloody best to make him regret it.

"Yes…" I whisper and then pass her the ring. I quickly throw it down on the table as the thought of touching it knocks me sick. To know what could have been had he not been thinking with his knob really tears me apart inside. We could have had everything and so much more.

Rachel's unusually quiet while she reads Tyler's letter, but I just leave her to it. There's no point in trying to discuss something that you can't change, is there? Especially something that you have no control over. "It's all a bit too little, too late , isn't it? I don't know what he's trying to achieve by doing this to you. Does he not know that he's hurt you enough?"

"According to his letter, he says he does."

"Words Emily, those are meaningless, empty words. You know as well as I do that actions speak a hell of a lot louder and his actions showed that he didn't give a crap about you anymore." She says flatly and even though it hurts hearing her say it, I know that she's right and I'd tell her exactly the same thing if the shoe was on the other foot. "You've come on brilliantly since he left. Please do not let this low-life make you go back there all because he finally felt the need to clear his conscience. He is not your problem anymore."

"I know. I know it's stupid that I'm still getting upset by it all, I just didn't expect him to send something like that."

"I know. But, now you have read it and heard what he's had to say, you can burn this and continue getting on with your life. To start with, you can wipe those beautiful eyes and get changed."

"Why?"

"Because I said so, and I really need a drink or five. Plus, the fresh air will do you the world of good."

She's right and I know it, but it doesn't make it any easier knowing that I'm about to face the world right after my heart has been shattered again.

Before I have a chance to say anything further, my best friend grabs me by the hand and pulls me to my feet "I'm not sure. I've got a bad feeling about this." I murmur, trying to find a way to get out of this.

"Oh, give over, do you seriously think that there could be anything worse than the crap you've had to go through today? No, I didn't think so."

Finally, after what feels like an age, I look a little bit presentable. I think? I've not got the energy to get all done up so instead I decided on my favourite pair of jeggings, a nice floaty blue top and some flats. Well, It's not like I'm going on a mad night out, just the pub down the road and there's nobody that I need to impress in there. That is, unless I change my mind, get absolutely reckless and cop off with one of the old guys. Yes, they're lovely to talk to, but saggy balls and erectile disfunction don't do anything to get my juices flowing.

"We're going to have a good night and pretend that today didn't happen. We'll cover everything that we need to tomorrow, okay?"

"Uh-huh." I say positively and I don't even convince myself. I'd love to be able to switch off, but my emotions are completely all over the show. I wonder if this is what it feels like when you go through the menopause. Maybe some HRT could help me out a little bit.

It doesn't surprise me to find our local haunt empty. It's a week night and most people prefer to drink in these days. All those weirdo's all loved up, it makes me feel sick. I know I'm bitter and deep down I'm only jealous, but still. On a plus note, I guess it means we can have a few drinks in peace and I don't need to worry about embarrassing myself if I end up having a nervous breakdown.

"What you having, your usual?" I ask Rachel as she hops into a booth, a nice quiet one secluded away from prying eyes, but we still have a good view of everything and everyone around us. This is our spot.

Every time we come here, it's always empty, as if it's reserved for us on a permanent basis.

"Yes, but make it two."

"How about four." Tonight, I plan on taking Rachel's advice and forgetting about everything by getting that shit faced, everything becomes a distant memory.

"Evening my love." Jade, the landlady welcomes me as I approach the bar. "I've not seen you in here on a school night for a while. Everything okay?"

"It will be." I plaster on my fake smile and she nods at me sympathetically. Clearly my make-up hasn't covered up my feelings as much as I'd hoped, or my puffy eyes. "You should probably get used to us holing ourselves up this place for a little while."

"That bad? Well, it's good business for me and you know that you and Rachel are welcome here anytime."

"Thanks, I appreciate it. In that case, I'll have two bottles of house white." This is just the start and I've already had one bottle back at home. Tonight could get messy, but do I care? Do I buggeries. A stonking hangover will be the distraction that I need to take my mind of my crappy life tomorrow.

Chapter 26

"So, how did things go with Doug?"

"Are you sure you want to talk about men right now?" Rachel eyes me cautiously and a real, genuine smile breaks free over my face. Oh, it feels weird, a little uncomfortable. My face must have been miserable for a lot longer than I originally thought.

"I don't mind talking about your man. Fuck the rest, but yours is still on my good list so he's okay. Well, depending on what you tell me anyway." I pick up my glass and sip a little as I wait for her to give me some good news at last. If it's not good news, then there's no hope for any of us ever again.

"It went… okay."

"Okay? Bloody hell Rach, you either sorted it out or you both decided to go your separate ways." I say bluntly. Harsh? Yes, but you have to be with Rachel sometimes, otherwise she'll be here all night going around the bloody houses and never once getting to the point. Plus, she doesn't think twice when she's being harsh to me.

"I think we're going to make it work."

"You are? That's great news. Now are you glad I made you take the plunge, or are you glad I made you take the plunge?"

"All right, yes, thank you." I love how I can give perfect advice to everyone around me, but I'm yet to master listening to any of my own. "I finally found the courage to tell him how I felt and what do you know, to my relief he said he felt the same. I'm super happy."

"What the hell did you ring me for then? You should have stayed with him you daft mare."

"Don't be daft, he's at mine anyway. I just had this urge to call you and I'm bloody glad I did. Anyway, don't you worry about him, he's got enough to keep him occupied while I'm away. You will always come first and if ever there comes a time where he doesn't understand that, then I'm afraid he's a goner. Love or not."

"Thank you. I really don't know what I'd do without you."

"I know. That's why I'm giving you the day off tomorrow to adjust to your new life."

"Excuse me, you're what?" I ask her, full of confusion. She's giving me the day off? From what?

"Do you really think that I'm just going to sit back and watch you suffer? That's not what friends do Emily. No, you'll be working for me until you don't need to anymore. Plus, it'll be fun." She smiles and my eyes grow wide in shock.

Fun? She calls that fun? "You really don't have to…" Please God, make her change her mind. There's no way that I can possibly work with her. I love coffee and I love Rachel, but combining the two solidly for eight hours or more on a daily basis could be pretty challenging.

"Don't look like that. I'll give you your space and you can work whatever hours you need. I just won't see you without a job and I most definitely will not just sit back and allow you to sign onto the dole when you don't need to."

"You promise that you won't boss me around? I don't think I'd be able to cope if you became power hungry."

"Piss off. What do you take me for? I promise, it won't even feel like you're working."

"Okay, well thank you. I'm telling you though, if you start bossing me around then I'll be walking right down to the job centre and I'll make you come with me, understand?" I warn and I know that she'd absolutely hate the idea of me doing that.

"Loud and clear, treacle. Loud and clear." A huge mega-watt grin lights up her whole face and another smile escapes me.

"Get to bed. You have got to be kidding me." Rachel slurs as she looks over my head, towards the bar. My head turns to look behind me and my eyes follow her line of sight. Are you kidding me? This is my local. What the hell does she think she's doing here?

Cruella. Cruella de bitch walking into my local. You honestly couldn't make this shit up.

As if her evil powers sense me, she turns her head towards me, her long mane of shabby extensions whipping down her back and she gives me a sly smile. One that says 'oh, I've been waiting to see you.'

"Is she coming over here?" Rachel hisses. "She bloody is as well, isn't she?"

Sure enough I look back at her and she's walking right towards our booth, drink in one hand and designer clutch in the other. She doesn't fit in here and boy does she stick out like a sore thumb.

"Emily..." She says, like butter wouldn't melt. "Well, this is the last place that I ever imagined bumping into you."

"You and me both. I would have thought that this little shin-dig would have been too much of a lower class for someone like you?" Rachel coughs to my side and almost spits her drink. I wish she would have, because it would have gone all over Cruella's lovely designer dress that no doubt cost more than my monthly wage. Well, my old monthly wage, anyway.

"It would be usually." She replies, still looking smug and not afraid to hold back. "But I'm meeting someone here, so what can you do?"

"Jump off the nearest fucking cliff?" My devil's back and for once he's picked a perfect time to come out and play.

"Sometimes you just have to come right down to their level and see what they're comfortable with. What's the word for it, compromise?"

"Something like that."

"I bet you're gutted, aren't you?" She continues, feigning deep concern, but I can see right through her. "I spoke to Daddy earlier and he told me everything that had happened. I have to tell you that he's pretty cut up about it all. Out of every single one of his employees, he always thought that it was you that he could always rely on and trust."

Why does she seem to think that this concerns her? It's got nothing to do with her, nothing at all. "That never changed. Someone set all of this up, I'm certain of it." I watch to see if her reaction changes, but I wouldn't be able to tell through all of that Botox that she has shoved in her face, courtesy of the bank of Daddy.

"I guess it's a mighty shame that it's a little too late to find out then, isn't it?" She draws her hair back from her face and her smug grin is still there, fixed firmly in place. "On a plus note though, I'm quite sure you'll fit right in at the job centre. Unfortunately for you, you probably won't get a decent job again. After all, what was it you were done for, sexual harassment and fraud? Scum like you belong on the dole."

"What did you just say?" That stupid little bitch.

I don't know why we both hate each other so much, but I do know that I wouldn't even piss on her if she was on fire. No, the hidden sadistic bitch buried within me would happily sit back and watch .I'm pretty certain that the feeling is mutual, too.

"Just look at yourself. You're nothing but a dirty little slapper. Always trying to work yourself around the office..."

I'm out of my seat before Rachel has a chance to pull me back down and my hand gives her a very loud and hard high five to the face. As the bar is still quite empty, give or take a few locals, the sound echoes out all around us and I can feel a number of heated stares burning into me. For once though, I really couldn't give too hoots. This evil bitch has had that coming for a long time.

After a couple of seconds, the drama queen in her comes out in full force. Cruella lifts her hand and protectively holds her face as she turns on the spot, circling the bar and playing the victim. "Did you see that?" She shouts? "Did you see how this crazy loon just attacked me for no reason. Someone call the police. Don't just sit there." She turns to me and the says, "I always knew you were a messed up cow."

"You have got to be joking?" I look back towards Rachel and all she can do is stare back at me disbelievingly. "The police?" I say, now focusing my attention back on Cruella. "You'll need more than the bloody police by the time I'm finished with you."

She turns on her heels slightly, so that only me and Rachel can see her. "I don't really think that would be a wise move, do you? You've already got fraud and sexual harassment on record, I don't think you need anything else. God, I'm so glad that I finally made Daddy see you for who you really are."

Then it clicks. Every last little piece of the puzzle slowly falls into place and connects seamlessly. "It was you? All this was you?" I launch for her again, wanting nothing more than to rip those cheap, tacky extensions from her bloody stupid and deluded head.

"Uh-huh." She grins back at me, not a single ounce of remorse running through her body. Actually, she looks super pleased with herself. "Come on Emily. Did you really think that I'd just sit back and listen to Daddy singing your praises all the time? Emily this... Emily that... I'm his daughter, not you. That business is rightfully mine and if I hadn't have stepped in when I did, he would have given it all to you. That's something that I wasn't going to allow to happen. Ever."

"You evil, vindictive little bitch."

"It was about time someone took you out of the equation. Just watching you throw yourself at Matt was sickening." *Matt?* What the hell does Matt have to do with any of this? "You know he doesn't even like you. He can't stand the sight of you at the best of times."

Wow. Just... wow.

Out of all of these revelations that are now coming to light, that's the one that hurts me the most. Matt. Who is she to make comments on Matt's behalf? She doesn't even know him. At least not like I do. I feel Rachel's hand on my arm as she tries to coax me back down into the booth, but I refuse to back down. I will stand my ground here. There's no way that I'm going to let a creature like her ruin my life any more than she already has. "Emily, she's not worth it. Look at her, she's desperate to get some kind of reaction out of you just so she can say 'I told you so,' to Daddy dearest." Rachel whispers.

"I'm out of a job. My career's ruined all because you've got some messed up Daddy issues?"

"Pretty much." She shrugs at me with no emotion in her body at all, apart from the wicked, evil smile. There's so much that I want to scream at her, and I'm about to get right to it, but my heart stops when I see a familiar figure walk towards us.

"There you are..." He says without paying much attention to his surroundings. "I'll grab a couple of drinks. What are you having?"

You have got to be having a bloody laugh. I can't move and I'm finding it harder and harder to breathe with each slow moment that passes. I want to look away, but I'm stood frozen to the spot as I'm forced to watch this sick and twisted scene play out right in front of me. Cruella knows how much this is affecting me. I can see it written in her eyes. She gives me one last smug smile, before turning around slowly to greet her guest.

She wastes no time by placing her twisted, dirty little hands on those beautiful, manly biceps before leaning up on her toes to grace him with an all too familiar peck on the cheek.

Little bitch. If I wanted to tie her up and torture her before, then it's got shit all on what I want to do to her right now.

Cruella makes sure that she pulls away from him as slowly as possible, ensuring that I get a whole view of the scene before me, and that's when he sees me... really sees me. His body stiffens instantly and his eye grow wide in shock. "Emily?"

"Fuck you, Matt." I snap and without thinking about anything else, I quickly turn around and make a dash for it, heading straight out of the bar and I don't even think about waiting for Rachel. I can't bring myself to turn around to see if she's following me, as I can't bring myself to look at him anymore.

The hurt that's rippling through my body is indescribable. What's going on? Why am I allowing him to get to me like this?

Chapter 27

Any minute now I'll wake up from this ridiculous nightmare that I've found myself in. I've got no idea what it is that I've done so bad to have all this shit hurled at me from different angles. No matter where I go, or what I do, it just doesn't seem to let up and something new keeps cropping up and slapping me in the face.

Ugh, I feel physically sick at the thought of Cruella and Matt together. It's just wrong on so many levels. I mean you wouldn't put beans and ice-cream together, it would be vile and that's exactly what the two of them are when they're together. Bloody vile.

"Emily… Emily stop." I hear Matt call out behind me. What the hell does he think he's playing at? I've just told him to do one and now he's running after me as if that's what I want.

"No I bloody don't want that. I just want him to leave me alone."

"No, you don't. This is exactly what you want. You want him to run after you, pull you close and tell you just how sorry he is and that everything will be okay."

"Piss off. Are you on crack?" I'm really going to need to have a serious talk with my head. Not only does it pipe up at the most irrelevant times, it's now babbling absolute tosh.

"Do one Matt. She clearly doesn't want to speak to you, or are you a thick piece of shit too?" Rachel screams at him like a crazed woman in the middle of the street. God, you've got to love Rachel. She's always got my back, no matter what. At least now I know that she followed me out. To be fair, I had it envisioned in my mind that she'd still be in be inside giving Cruella a right good talking too. I guess it looks like I'll have to wait for that day to come.

"Emily just stop. Please…" He pleads over Rachel's loud vocals. "It's not what it looks like?"

That's it. I stop and spin like a mad woman in the middle of the street and stare him down. How dare he come at me and say crap like that. How dare he even try to speak to me after ditching me as soon as he got his knob wet. Yes, we may have had a drunken fumble, but above everything, I thought we were friends. But we can't be friends if he dropped me at the first hurdle.

Oh no, he didn't need to worry about me, as it seems that he was too busy keeping Cruella warm. God, he knows how much I hate her too. Total knob.

Unable to contain myself any longer, I walk towards him, an unfamiliar feeling building deep within my chest. Why am I even letting him get to me like this? Why do I feel so much more than anger towards him? "I don't give a shit what it looks like Matthew." I hiss as soon as I'm close enough for him to hear me "It's no concern of mine what you do with your time."

"Emily, come on, don't be a dick."

"Don't be a dick? Have you even stopped to listen to yourself? I thought you were my friend? Or did that end as soon as you got what you wanted?" I snap back, unable to contain my anger and hurt. I feel violated and humiliated and he's just rubbed salt in my wounds by hooking up with her.

"It's just a drink…"

"I'm not arsed. Honestly, give your head a wobble and get over yourself."

"I've been trying to get a hold of you." He says, his eyes growing wide as he pleads with me to listen to him.

"Yeah?" I say, disbelievingly. "Well, you clearly didn't try hard enough, did you?"

"I really need to talk to you… about stuff."

"No, no you don't. Me and you, we're done. I never took you to be that type of guy, yet here you are…"

"Matt, come back inside." Cruella calls out as she hobbles out of the pub. She's lucky that I'm so angry at Matt, otherwise nothing would stop me from storming over to her and hurting her as much as physically possible.

"Best go running back to your girlfriend. Wouldn't want to keep your precious princess waiting, would you? Oh… and just so you know. I got sacked today, not that you give a crap, but I did. So, I'm now without a job all because of your new fuck buddy." Matt watches me with a blank expression as if everything that I've just said to him is in a foreign language. "What, don't believe me? Why don't you go and ask her?"

Matt doesn't say anything, he just looks at me like he's lost, but I'm not falling for his bullshit routine. I've been through enough recently and he knows it. I don't need any more negativity in my life.

All that's left for me to do is to walk away from it all. What's another heartbreak? The rate things are going, I'm becoming quite the pro at dealing with them. Maybe I should start an online problem page. Steering the innocent untarnished hearts away from it all before it's much too late.

Chapter 28

My heads sore and my eyes hurt. Oh God, everything hurts so bad. Why, oh why did I think it would be a good idea to neck another bottle of wine when I got home? My bloody liver is going to pack in on me and then what am I going to do?

You really need to get your life in order, Parker. Asap.

I try to move over on my side, but my brain doesn't want to function with my muscles. I haven't got a clue what time it is. To be fair, I don't even know what time I passed out. It must have been late, but saying that, I don't really remember much after throwing up my empty stomach into the kitchen sink around midnight, only to fill it up again with alcohol. It's not big and it's not clever.

How did yesterday even happen? Everything starts filtering through my mind, flashing before me, replaying over and over again. As if my hangover wasn't bad enough, now I've got to contend with everything that went to pot yesterday.

"Do you really want to spend the rest of your life living like this? Wallowing in self-pity and stale body odour?"

I couldn't think of anything worse. It's like I've become a shadow of my former self. There was a time when I wouldn't even dream of leaving the house without freshly ironed clothes and a face full of flawless make-up. Now, I'm no make-up artist, but it's amazing what a couple of you-tube tutorials can do.

No, enough is enough. Today is the day that I'm going to try and get my life back on track. If I remember correctly I've even got a job to go to tomorrow, too. Oh, the joys. Hopefully Rachel will go easy on me. I've warned her about being pushy so I really hope that she takes that on board.

Yes, today everything that I do will be positive and I'm really going to try my best to become a better person. Sod everyone who has tried to drag me down. I don't need those kinds of people in my life. But, first things first, it's time I had a shower and stuffed my mush with something greasy.

Priorities.

After speaking to Rachel earlier, I feel a lot better. From what she said I didn't really do anything to make a tit out of myself. Apparently she was pretty proud of me for finally standing my ground and sticking up for myself. Honestly, I'm pretty proud of me too, I never knew that I had it in me.

I've decided that today is going to be a whole day dedicated to me, team Emily. I plan on doing nothing other than spending my last day of unemployment curled up on the couch watching Gilmore Girls and nothing and no one is going to stop me. Well, maybe a couple of bars of Galaxy.

I can hear my phone buzzing to life somewhere on the couch, but I haven't got the energy to find it. Sod it, if it's important then they'll either call back or leave a message. I'm perfectly happy slouching it out like the true sloth that I am and I wouldn't really be doing myself any favours by moving. This could be my last day of peace for God knows how long. I fully intend to enjoy it.

My eyes grow heavy as a knock sounds at the front door. Jesus, all I wanted was some peace and quiet for one day. Guess it doesn't look like I'm going to get it though. I'm tempted to leave it, but last time it was Rachel and she almost took my door off. Obviously, I don't want that to happen again. The last thing I want to happen is Mr. Jones having a heart attack.

Reluctantly I pull my mahoosive arse up and off the couch and head towards the front door. Whoever it is, it better be worth it. It's not often that I pause something. Now I kind of understand how Rachel feels when she's disturbed from watching Geordie Shore.

"Oh, hey."

"Hi." I say, surprised to find Noah stood on my door step. "How are you?"

"I'm good." He smiles and he looks so carefree. "I hope you don't mind me just turning up like this? Rachel gave me your address."

"Oh, she did?" Wait until I see her tomorrow. Yes, she probably thought that she was doing me a favour, but my heads so mashed with everything that's happened, Noah is the last person that I wanted to see. I look down, a little embarrassed at my choice of outfit. Oh well, he better love penguins. "Sorry, come in." I step aside to allow him to pass, and my mind automatically wanders back to when Matt last came over.

Jesus, why can't I get him out of my head?

"I thought I'd come and see you after you had to dash off the other night. I would have called but I figured you might have enjoyed the surprise more?"

Wrong. I hate surprises. Even Matt knows how much I hate surprises. One thing he was always good at was keeping me away from them. But, that was then…

I look at Noah and smile at him. My God he really is beautiful. Before I have chance to say anything further, he's on me, his lips possessively seeking mine. My body reacts automatically and I can't help but follow his lead. Our tongues glide against each other, slowly at first and then Noah starts to pick up the pace a little. I try my best to follow suit, but something isn't right. It feels completely wrong and I don't know why.

I pull back a little, and I'm unable to meet his gaze. "Sorry… too much, too soon?" he asks.

Emily, don't be a dick here. Just look at him for God sake. I shake my head at him and lean up again on my toes to reach him. As my lips touch his again, I wait to feel something. A spark, a connection, but there is nothing there. Nothing except the image of Matt every time I close my eyes.

Oh no. No, no, no. This cannot be happening. Not after everything that's happened.

"I'm sorry Noah." I say, as soon as everything connects in my head. "I can't do this. I'm just not ready…" I hope he doesn't think that I've been leading him on, because I haven't been. I genuinely do find him attractive in every way possible. But that's as far as it goes. He doesn't make my heart pound, he doesn't make me laugh the way Matt does and he definitely doesn't drive me around the bend like Matt does.

For God sake, why has it taken me so long to see what's been right in front of me all this time?

Matt... It's always been Matt.

"No, that's fine. I completely get it. Maybe coming over wasn't such a great idea after all?" He asks. "Look, I don't want to make you feel any more uncomfortable than you already do, so I'll go. But, if you change your mind or you fancy doing something, well, you've got my number so give me a call."

I'm quite surprised how that went. Noah took it a lot better than I did. Well, why wouldn't he? He's probably got a long line of girls to choose from so he's not really going to miss me all that much. Me on the other hand, I feel shocking. I feel like I've led him on a merry-go-round and that was never my intention. Bloody hell none of this was.

Now, I'm faced with a massive problem A problem that I don't know how to solve. To tell you the truth, I haven't even got a clue where to start with it all.

How do I tell Matt how I feel? Should I even tell him how I feel? There's probably no point as I can just imagine him and Cruella getting all cosy and no doubt laughing at my expense.

Maybe I should give Rachel a call. She'll know just what to do. But then, she'd probably chew my ears off about how shocking he's been. I can't lie, if I do end up speaking to him again, I'll personally remind him just how shocking he's been.

Knock... Knock... Knock...

Oh no. Obviously, Noah didn't take it as lightly as I thought. Either that or he's coming back for his phone. Shit, I didn't even think about that. But, I'm a proud girl and I'd never stay with someone over a gift. Even an iPhone.

"I'm sorry... "I begin as soon as I open the door, unable to raise my eyes to meet Noah's face. God, I'm such a coward.

"Me too." My eyes shoot upwards at the sound of that voice. A voice that I didn't think I would be hearing for a while.

"Matt?" I say, part shock and part happiness. "What are you doing here?" I need to remember that I'm still mad at him and I don't want him to think that I'm about to let him off the hook so easily. Matt doesn't answer me, instead, for the second time in the space of thirty minutes I'm enveloped in someone's embrace, only this time I don't hesitate. I allow him to claim me like I did before, only this time I have no intention of letting him go, ever.

"It's always been you Emily Parker. I've fucking loved you from the minute you stepped foot into that office when you turned my world upside down. I'm done with messing around. I'm fed up of playing games."

"You are?" I ask, full of disbelief. "What happened last time? You walked away without so much as a goodbye."

"I know, I'm a dick..."

"Too bloody right you are." I laugh. "Where's Cruella?"

"There's never been anything going on between us two. Sure, she's tried it on a couple of times, but I've always blew her off. After last night, she was ruthless and told me everything that she'd done to set you up. I'm guessing she thought that I'd be happy about it and hang out the flags for her or something? There's no way that I can associate with someone like that. Forgive me?" He pleads and gently takes my face in his hands, bringing his face closer to mine before placing his lips on mine once again. This time he doesn't pull away, instead he holds me tight as he walks us both back into the house without breaking our embrace.

"We'll see…" I say, as I pull away and lean back briefly. "You've got a hell of a lot of making up to do Matthew."

"Now that sounds like music to my ears. I've also emailed Graham with everything that happened, including some video footage from someone from the bar too. With any luck, you'll be back tomorrow and Amanda will be gone."

"Thanks, it means a lot that you'd do that for me, but honestly, I can't go back and work for someone who let me down and treated me like that. I just can't do it."

Never in the history of man did I think that Matt would mean this much to me. It's crazy to think that it's taken all of this drama for me to see that what I've wanted and needed all along was sitting right in front of me and this time I'm going to hold on tight and never let go. I will make it my mission to keep the communication going and to questions things when they don't feel right.

Well, that's if I survive to get that far. I've still got to see Rachel and I know that she's going to have quite a lot of colourful words to say on this whole matter and in my ecstatic state, I'm looking forward to each and every single one of them.

Be sure to keep your eyes peeled for updates on the next book...

Emily and Rachel WILL be back with some more adventures in the not too distant future.

ACKNOWLEDGEMENTS

I have absolutely loved living in Emily Parker's world and I hope you do too. Not only is she fun and a little bit crazy, but she's a good girl at heart with a lot of love to give when she's given half the chance.

Firstly, I'd like to thank Louise. Not only is she a fabulous PA, but she's also a dab hand at swag making and keeping me sane. She's also amazing when it comes to whipping me into shape too. Thank you Louise, for everything you do for me. It's very much appreciated.

I'd also like to say a massive thank you to you, my readers, new and also to you who have been with me since the very beginning. You're support means everything to me and it still blows me away that you read and escape off into the worlds that I create.

Lastly, thank you to my nearest and dearest for always supporting me in all that I do. Even putting up with me randomly busting out one-liners. I know you all love it really.

Until the next one...

Much love,

Steph xx

Printed in Great Britain
by Amazon